Praise for

THE BLUE DOOR

"When you step through *The Blue Door*, Janice Deal invites you into a world both ordinary and extraordinary, where magic weaves through the fabric of daily life. At its heart is Flo, a wandering spirit and unconventional seeker, whose quest to unravel a shattering family tragedy leaves her estranged, misunderstood, yet fiercely resilient. . . . Deal masterfully blends the mundane with the mythical, creating a tale that lingers long after the final page."

—**Julie E. Justicz**, author of *Conch Pearl* and *Degrees of Difficulty*

"This seemingly simple story of a woman trying to come to terms with her daughter's horrendous crime turns into an otherworldly reflection on how to be in the world and what matters—and it is deeply moving and marvelous in every sense of the word."

—**Ellen Akins**, author of *Home Movie, World Like a Knife*, and others

"Flo's humility and quiet courage, not to mention her capacity for endurance, make for a thrilling read. As she propels herself through the bright, parched desert city, her story, both past and future, takes on the shimmer of a truly magical spiritual journey. Charles Baxter once said, 'You must love your characters, and visit trouble upon them,' and Janice Deal does exactly that, with pitch-perfect tenderness, humor and clarity. Flo is unforgettable, and the climax of the story is both surprising and inevitable. A beauty of a novel."

—**Marjorie Sandor**, author of *The Secret Music at Tordesillas*

"*The Blue Door* is about finding one's place in the world while life keeps adding up. With her signature grace and merciful eye, Deal sticks a glorious, complicated landing where next steps beckon."

—**James Magruder**, author of *Vamp Until Ready*

"The poetry of this novel delighted me. In transparent, unpretentious prose, Janice Deal taps the visceral peril of parenthood—how the role of Mother envelops and entraps the former self, how a creator is enmeshed with her creation—from this side of a beckoning blue door that opens onto an alternate life."

—**Elizabeth Mosier**, author of *Excavating Memory: Archaeology and Home*

"*The Blue Door* weaves together past, present, future with a potent fairy tale . . . to create a luminous story that is heartbreaking, full of heart, and unforgettable."

—**Lynn Sloan**, author of the novels *Midstream* and *Principles of Navigation* and the story collection *This Far Isn't Far Enough*

"In *The Blue Door*, we follow the stalwart Flo on a memorable and, at times, mystical quest for comfort and connection. I was gripped by every step of Flo's journey, but especially her brave willingness to confront the darkness of the past in the hope of emerging on the other side. Never has Janice Deal's writing been deeper or more luminous."

—**Katherine Shonk**, author of *The Red Passport* and *Happy Now?*

"At the heart of the novel is Flo, a mother navigating grief, regret, and longing as she prepares for a reunion with her estranged and troubled daughter, Teddy. Flo's physical journey throughout the story, to find her missing dog, mirrors an inner pilgrimage, turning a simple walk through a desert town into a profound exploration of the human condition. The people she encounters along the way and her memories—both uplifting and unsettling—add texture to her journey, while the echoes of an old family folktale infuse the narrative with a timeless, almost mythic resonance. With spare and evocative prose, Deal perfectly captures the harsh beauty of the desert landscape and the rich emotional terrain of her protagonist."

—**Kate Brandes**, author of *Stone Creek* and *The Promise of Pierson Orchard*

"In Janice Deal's mercurial meditation on the power of language and story, one woman's quest for her lost dog through a desert town becomes an epic adventure. With delightful prose and rich characterization Deal renders the quotidian with an acuity that charms these pages to life: walking sticks are wizard staffs, dogs are gods, and blue doors offer passageways to alternate worlds. Yet when ghosts of memory weigh as heavily as the desert heat, how does one find grace, forgiveness, and hope in a world beset with relentless reminders of our past pain? Open *The Blue Door* to find a way."

—**Jeremy T. Wilson**, author of *The Quail Who Wears the Shirt* and *Adult Teeth*

"It is a mother's challenge to let her child go into the world and find a separate life. But what if that child has committed a savage crime, forcing this separation? 'I am your blind spot,' Teddy says to her mother, Flo. . . . Over the space of a day, Flo embarks on a quest to find her dog while meditating on love and forgiveness, on loneliness and connection. In this beautiful short novel, Janice Deal leaves us thunderstruck yet hopeful in the face of despair."

—**Jan English Leary**, author of *Town and Gown*, *Skating on the Vertical*, and *Thicker Than Blood*

THE BLUE DOOR

a **WalkAbout** book

OTHER BOOKS BY JANICE DEAL

Strange Attractors: The Ephrem Stories

The Sound of Rabbits

The Decline of Pigeons: Stories

THE BLUE DOOR

a novel

Janice Deal

NEW DOOR BOOKS
Philadelphia 2025

New Door Books
An imprint of P. M. Gordon Associates, Inc.
2115 Wallace Street
Philadelphia, Pennsylvania 19130
U.S.A.

Cover photograph from iStock.com
Cover design by John Hensler

Library of Congress Control Number: 2024949846
ISBN 978-1-7355585-7-8 (paperback)
ISBN 978-1-7355585-8-5 (e-book)

In memory of Mary Jo Kanady

(1942–2024)

For David

A fable! A fable! Bring it!

(Kanuri)

OR

A story, a story. Let it go, let it come.

(Traditional West African opening)

PART ONE

1

THE DAY STILL felt naïve. Was that it? Perhaps Flo meant hopeful. She would like to be hopeful. Although usually, for Flo, hope lived next to its absence. Always the two, together.

Sunby used to like those opposites. "Darkness was over the surface of the deep," he would say. "Then the light came," he always added. He was no Pollyanna, Sunby, but he believed that this day—*this!*—might be anything.

Most of Flo's days are the same. Today will be different, but Flo doesn't know this yet. For now there is the reassuring clap of the cats, coming through the narrow cat door after their nightly prowl. Last night Flo had alertly listened for the sound of their return, but she has learned to sleep through uncertainty. They're okay, she finally told herself. After a while, she had drifted off.

This morning she makes tea before walking, the kettle rolling.

Flo is thinking about Teddy. Flo often thinks about her daughter, although she doesn't always know what to think and she tells herself she does not miss Teddy anymore. For a long time, Flo missed the little girl Teddy had been. And when Teddy was sent away, the missing was like physical pain.

After Teddy went to Juvie, Flo had moved to be near her. She called the town JuvieLand, her own name for the place, and so long as Teddy was there it was Flo's home. Sleepless, she would drive to the Juvie gates in the middle of the night. Other cars were there in the darkness also, engines idling. Most contained a single occupant. Most of these drivers were women. Mothers, presumably. Or grandmothers. Sisters or aunts. Flo never spoke to these women, she didn't have to. They were all marking time until things lightened up.

She'd called her ex-husband, Charlie, early on. This was during the trial, when the people of Ephrem had decided what they'd decided: that Teddy was a monster, that Flo was the monster who'd made her.

"They're wrong about her. She's okay, right?" Flo could sense his shrug over the phone.

"You wanted to be the parent," he said. "You wanted her for yourself." There was a pause; she could hear the scratch of a match, she heard his wheezy suck on a cigarette. There would be whiskey too, Flo guessed. He hadn't quit, as he'd promised to do years ago when Teddy was born. "Nice job," he said.

She'd called him for reassurance, or to share the blame. But Charlie had clearly cut them loose, revenge (Flo supposed) for the way they'd left him. *She'd* left him.

Sometime during the JuvieLand years, the phone number Flo had for Charlie wasn't working anymore, and she reached out to Sunby; she asked him to help her locate Teddy's dad. Flo vaguely thought that Sunby's belief in God might elevate this effort, as if God would try harder to help a person like Sunby, a person with faith. But even Sunby couldn't find someone who was determined not to be found. It was as if Charlie had fallen off the face of the earth. Maybe he'd changed his name. Or maybe he'd died. People had a habit of doing that.

Flo knew.

When Teddy was first put away, Flo felt as though she were constantly falling; nothing was solid, nothing was what she had thought. Then things improved, if improvement meant adjusting to her only child having done what she'd done. The events of the evening Mrs. Benedict died (that's how Flo always thought of it, the woman *had* died, after all) receded into the past, along with the way life had been, good and bad both, before that day. Flo's New Normal became just Normal—whatever Normal was, as she once said to Sunby. There was comfort in this. Then after Teddy was released from Juvie, and moved on, Flo adjusted to how her daughter lived far away. She came to accept the way they communicated, which was sometimes.

That is Normal now.

This is how Flo makes tea: she fills the teapot and her cup halfway each with hot water from the kettle. She swirls the water in her cup, to warm it, then dumps the water out.

She spoons three teaspoons of Assam into the pot and adds more hot water. She steeps the tea for three minutes, watching the clock and thinking about the tea leaves unfurling. Then she adds powdered cream. She likes what she likes.

Also, she slices up a pear. The pear is for her ulcer; she never ate them before. The doctor she saw when she lived in JuvieLand said she got ulcers because of her smoking. He didn't know about the business with Teddy and Mrs. Benedict, but after that was when the ulcers came. Flo stopped smoking anyway. This wasn't easy, but it was something she could do. And she has learned to love the pears, or at least like them.

Mrs. Benedict: what happened was that Teddy bashed her teacher's head in with a piece of fiber cement trim. But Flo thinks of what happened as "the business," or maybe "the incident." All semantics, she thinks, though she cannot persuade herself to call it an accident. As Teddy has.

"Hey, now," she greets the animals, who crowd her as she makes her tea, as she eats her slice of pear. There are four cats, including SilverGirl. There is the dog. She distractedly reaches down and rubs SilverGirl's ear. She scratches Dog under the chin. She scratches her own shoulder, her neck. Now she is thinking about Sunby, who has died—just days ago back in Ephrem, Illinois—so that thinking of him, it hurts.

His was an April death.

She will need to tell Teddy about Sunby, and in her head Flo shies away: from the death, from the telling.

Using a strainer, Flo pours tea into her rainbow mug, the one Teddy painted before she was old enough to be ironic. When she was still young enough that her gifts were bestowed adoringly. When she still gave gifts at all.

Flo *had* been adored, once.

As she takes a sip, mail rattles through the slot, hitting the floor; sometimes it comes early, before the day's worst heat. It's already Wednesday and Flo meant to give the mail carrier her check for the electric bill, so she sets the tea aside, she runs to the door and flings it wide. "Wait!" she cries, and the carrier, a friendly-enough woman with braids and tiny square sunglasses, stands patiently, shifting her mail sack to the other shoulder while Flo runs back inside and retrieves the check in its envelope.

"Thank you!"

"Sure sure," the woman says, then dips her head to the right. "I think your dog got out. He run around the side there?"

"Dog. Right," Flo says. Her front door hangs open, her feet are bare. Flo scratches at her neck again. "I'll put on some shoes and get him."

Back inside she scoops up the mail. There are more bills, a flyer for a new sushi place, the usual junk. And there's an envelope addressed to Flo in Teddy's unmistakable slanty hand.

Teddy! Flo tears open the envelope. Teddy's latest letter is a notecard; on the front of it is a photo of a goat in a bathtub. Flo breathes in, then out. She examines the image on the front. The goat has those weird goat eyes but it does not look unhappy.

She opens the card slowly and scans the beginning of Teddy's note. It seems her daughter is coming—to where Flo lives, that's what the first few lines say; Teddy doesn't call it home. This doesn't bother Flo. She doesn't call it home either. Flo believes Teddy when she says she will come: Teddy is private (some might say secretive, or sly), but when she *does* say something, it is the truth, or some version of it. Teddy's version of it, certainly, and if Flo once wished that Teddy would open up to her more, she was cured of that wish when Teddy . . .

Well.

Flo takes one more look at the card—"I could use some time with you, Flo," the second paragraph begins—then slips it into her skirt pocket. It's a long note, longer than Teddy has written in a while. Whether that's a good sign or a sign of trouble—depression, dislocation—Flo isn't sure. She doesn't know her child as well as she did, or thought she did. She wonders more and more often now if she even knows how to be Teddy's mother. Where you know what they need.

SilverGirl winds around her ankles and Flo gives her a distracted pat. "Yes yes, I'll call for Dog," she murmurs. "Don't worry now."

She has already made mistakes. Flo has. Gifts she bought Teddy—for her birthday, which is in July. For Christmas. The gifts were wrong, have been wrong for some time. Flo suspects that when Teddy moves to a new place, as she frequently does, she leaves behind the thick slippers shaped like unicorns, or the T-shirt from a podcast Teddy briefly liked in middle school. Sometimes, late at night, Flo torments herself, imagining Teddy leaving behind the dictionary Flo made by hand, with its definitions of the words Teddy and Flo created in a language all their own. Derrykin, the language was—Flo and Teddy came up with Derrykin together. Well, Teddy did, with her faculty for languages. She was so small, no more than nine years old, and yet this came easily to her, it seemed. Flo? She memorized the phonetics, the phrases, so that they could communicate, just the two of them.

"I made this for you, Mama," Teddy had said. She still called her Mama then. She'd been scribbling in a notebook, she was always filling notebooks with her thoughts, her drawings. This notebook, the Derrykin notebook, had a red cover, and Teddy produced it at dinner one night (Flo still remembers what they were eating: Salisbury steak). "This is something for just you and me." Inside lived a list of words and phrases; in her childish hand, Teddy had also written out rough phonetics.

The notebook is long gone. Flo doesn't know what became of it but it didn't matter: the two of them had long since internalized its contents. The dictionary Flo subsequently made was an homage, written on lumpy handmade paper with a fine ink pen. It was a labor of love; Flo even sketched illustrations! Cat. Ball. Horn. She wanted Teddy to remember what they once shared.

She has always given Teddy all she has. She sends the gifts.

Surely she will look forward to the visit from her daughter. But perhaps she will dread it, also.

SilverGirl is meowing. "I know," Flo says. "It's okay. Dog will come when I call him."

She thinks instinctively of Sunby, who would have something reassuring to say: about Teddy, about the visit. Who might sit with Flo, half a continent away, while she read Teddy's letter, all the way through, aloud over the phone. They would discover it together; with Sunby there, Flo would not be alone. But. That is the way it used to be. And there it is again: the missing, like a wound. Flo almost gasps; no-Sunby is not Normal, not yet.

She closes her eyes, then opens them. Her own mother's practicality asserts itself. "I'll find him," Flo says to Silver-Girl. She goes outside and calls for Dog, who isn't in the fenced side yard with its chain-link gate, which is broken and leans open (Flo has meant to tell the landlord about this). Dog has been here, he has left a grayness behind him. He hasn't been gone long. The dog is blocky, soft triangular ears planted high. His teeth are small and neat and very white.

It is unusual for him to go far without her. "Dog!" she cries again, because that is the name she has given him. "Hey!" In the still morning, her voice carries, but listen: it is not the only thing. There is the fizz of traffic also, those trucks. Flo lives in a small city, in a neighborhood near a commercial district that's sprung up along a four-lane road (sometimes called a *stroad*, Flo has learned). This early the light is still weightless, but she senses the hard heat of the day that is coming and this makes her tired. Sometimes the heat gives her headaches, and then her eyeballs feel like hot glass. But it is a dry heat, everyone says so.

Flo's voice is rusty. There is not much talk, the way she lives now, though things weren't always this way. Once, she was a social worker at a community college. She was almost garrulous then, open, in a way the students she worked with weren't or couldn't be. After the incident Flo became less open, too; looking back, she wonders if she's lost her true nature, or if this current self has been the truth all along, waiting to be declared.

She feels sympathy for Younger Flo, the way you would feel sympathy for someone you hardly know, even a stranger. And it's possible being alone has rendered her strange. Her animals accept her, in any case. Even the chickens she kept, back when she had chickens, had accepted her in their way. In Ephrem, this was.

If you've never lived alone, you don't know.

She calls for Dog, again and again and again.

Flo's apartment is in a house with one floor. There is no basement. There is no attic. This is a tract house made of concrete block and Flo has three rooms at the front: a living room, a bedroom, and her own bath with a molded plastic shower, no tub. There is a galley kitchen that is part of the living room, and the ceilings throughout are low; it is like living in an animal's den (this is not a bad thing, Flo thinks). Behind Flo's apartment is a second, smaller apartment—a studio, really. A woman named B. lives there; she is Flo's neighbor, and the closest thing Flo has to a friend in this town.

Both apartments have sliding doors that give out onto the patio, which is a concrete slab on the side of the house. The houses in Flo's neighborhood are set close together, and Flo supposes that a few of them are rentals as well, though she doesn't know of any other homes converted to apartments like this one. She counts herself lucky: she likes living in an apartment that feels like a house, with a proper front yard, even if that yard is just gravel. Flo's apartment has the scrap of side yard also, baked almost to stone with cracks running through it, all of it surrounded by the chain-link with its gate. (Flo asked her landlord to install a cat flap in her front door, and to her surprise he did. A lonely transplanted Greek with an exuberant head of hair, the landlord likes animals, he's nice enough.)

The side yard her landlord has created for the rental is ugly but clean, empty except for one dignified pencil cholla with its long spines pointing downwards. The animals know to stay away from it.

Flo walks through the broken gate and skirts the pencil cholla. The yard is tidy—she keeps it clear of animal waste—and B. has put out a concrete frog to "guard the place." Flo leans over and taps its head, she does this for luck. "Dog!" she calls. Her voice stronger. She thinks, as she often does, that she likes this yard that asks for nothing; it's enough to keep up with her apartment.

The apartment! Always the bunnies of dust. Always the fur, from the cats and Dog. Animals shed, it's what they do. She tries to keep the place clean as wheat but it is an effort. The older she gets, the less patience she has for such rituals: cleanliness for its own sake no longer interests or defines her the way it might once have. Besides, she is used to the puffs of fur, drifting across the tile floor.

In any case, no one but B. comes to her rooms. Flo sometimes imagines what it might be like to entertain friends here, as she never did when Teddy was small, when Flo might have had occasion for visitors: Teddy's friends, for instance, had there been any. Their pretty, friendly mothers.

Teddy will be her guest now.

Flo stands, chewing at her lip. There is Sunby. There is Dog. There is Teddy. Her mind beetles, distracted; she thinks about yesterday, stocking shelves at the upscale grocery called The Bounty, where she works. Flo privately calls it The Mutiny, as in *Mutiny on the Bounty*. This amuses her; Flo likes naming (re-naming) things. The store is located in the "nice" part of town, where the houses are bigger and people will pay $17 for a pound of coffee. The Mutiny stocks only the best.

Right now The Mutiny is carrying special decorative soaps, wrapped in paper so thick and textured it's like a gift. Yesterday Flo arranged the soaps reverently, meditatively: their sheer heft conveyed respectability. Maybe she will buy one of those clean-smelling bricks, she thinks now. Maybe she will buy one for her daughter's visit. Back in Ephrem, Flo used to buy soap in those hand pumps. Apparently everyone did; that's what she'd used to wash her own hands, again and again. At the police station. After the incident.

The paper towels had been cheap and scratchy.

She prefers bar soap now.

2

"DOG!" FLO CALLS again from the patio slab.

She slides her feet into the sandals she leaves near the patio door. They are cheap, each one a single molded piece of shiny plastic. Flo bought them because the color—red—cheered her. In certain lights the red sparkles, and the shoes are more comfortable than they look. Flo likes them even though when it rains the flat, gridded soles become slippery and skid across wet pavement. Then it is like being on skates. Or dancing by accident.

It used to be, they would line up their shoes: Charlie, Flo, Teddy. Big to small. Flo likes thinking of that. Being a family was real—scary but also fun. Flo and Charlie had been together for several years by the time Teddy came along; you would have thought they had it down, but the small pressures of sharing a life eventually became too much, for Flo and Charlie at least. For a time Teddy was the one thing Charlie and Flo both believed in, utterly. And for a time this was enough. They had created this being, and they raised her, together, as long as they could manage it. Then at a certain point Teddy became Flo's to raise, and damage, alone.

"Dog!" Flo pictures the things that could be going wrong for him: a truck with loose brakes, an angry coyote. So many boots in the world, just waiting to kick.

"Come!" she yells. Then she sighs. He can't have gone far. "I don't need this," Flo says out loud.

This is the part where Flo would have called Sunby. "Dog's just fine," Flo can almost hear him saying. Catching her lip between her teeth again, Flo hurries to her patio door. B. knows and loves Dog. She will know what to say also.

B's front door is the old back door of the house, and B. has her own sliding patio door, next to Flo's, but these are usually locked. There is also a way to get from one apartment to another through adjoining closets and the two women prefer this: it's like a secret passage.

"Dog!" Flo calls again over her shoulder. One more time. Then she goes into her apartment, and her head is roaring the way it can do.

Think, Flo tells herself. On the kitchen counter is a packaged muffin mix she brought home from The Mutiny yesterday, instead of the soap, the kind that you make in a cup or a mug, in the microwave. *When you don't know what to do, keep your hands busy,* Flo's mother used to say.

Flo makes the muffin.

It's an easy thing—just powdered mix and water—and Flo listens to the microwave purr, transforming nothing, really, into something. She drinks her cooling tea and listens to the plumbing, which is strange in the house. Sometimes there is the sound of running water. There is the sound of running water today. Sometimes the water sounds like the yipping of a dog. Flo used to wake and think that it was Dog, barking. It never was. Over time she has become used to the sounds and now they bring her solace. The sound of B. moving around at night—the walls of this place are very thin—is also a comfort.

B. is a comfort.

Flo heads to the closet, where she pushes through the wind pants and sweatshirts that hang like Spanish moss. She pushes aside the fiberboard panel, which B. has painted blue. B. chose the exact shade of blue based on stories Flo has told her, about a door, about the promise it holds. Flo recognized the love behind this gesture; she holds it close to her heart. Now she emerges into B's closet, then B's main living space, with the cup in her hand. It's like *Rosemary's Baby,* this passageway, only nice! The rule is that you call out if you take the passageway. Flo does this now.

"I'm here!" Flo cries. She feels the familiar, falling-away sensation at the back of her head. Like vertigo. As if it were all, already, too late. As if nothing she did going forward might make the least bit of difference. This is how it was when Teddy did what she did, all those years ago. Her daughter, destroyed. And also the destroyer: Teddy's jeans, her hands and face, branded with Mrs. Benedict's blood.

Flo tells herself that Dog is fine, that he'll probably be at the front door by the time she gives B. the muffin. Her own inadequacies won't be put to the test—not this time, not again.

"I have something for you!"

The room is tidy, bed already made. "Hello! Hello!" Flo calls. B., wearing pajama bottoms decorated with Santas and a T-shirt reading, *You Are the Piña to My Colada*, emerges from the bathroom. She comes and takes Flo's hands in hers. B. smells like soap, like clean things. Her supple face is powdered like a biscuit and has a child's sweetness in it.

B. *is* sweet. She is also broken and slow, and brings Flo animals to tend. In return, Flo puts drops in her eyes, because B. has the glaucoma. Flo also helps her friend write out checks to pay her bills, which aren't many. B. has a sister who takes care of her rent and makes sure she gets enough to eat. But Flo is B.'s friend, something B.'s sister is not. B. has never said this, but Flo, she knows the signs. And here is the thing: Flo is kind. She is good at reading people (besides Teddy). And she is fun to be with, or she was, when she put herself out into the world.

"Dog is gone," Flo says.

"Dog is on the town," B. says, relieving Flo of the still-warm mug. Her hands are deformed by arthritis. B. has told

Flo that she has learned to win people over because, as she says, folks don't like signs of aging. In themselves, in others. Even here in this town which skews so old.

"He must be visiting the blue hairs," B. laughs, and Flo, reassured, laughs also.

B. calls everyone else in town, people over a certain age, blue hairs, then likes to point out that she and Flo don't have the blue hair. Which makes them the opposite of old, of course. It's true that they don't dye their hair: Flo is indifferent to her salt and pepper, and B likes her veil of white. "Have I ever mentioned that I should have been a plastic surgeon?" (B. has, often, it's her joke.) "Wouldn't I be rich, living here and taking care of everyone's nips and tucks!"

She cackles again. People yearn to be something else, that's B.'s theory. They long to transform, as if stretching their skin tight might actually accomplish this. Spotted hands, a rumpled neck. So what?, B. says. Along with Sunby, B. is one of the most decent people Flo has known.

She puts her hand on Flo's arm and steers them both to the kitchenette. She sets the muffin next to the sink. "Sit," B. says, nodding at the one chair. Then she hoists herself onto the kitchen worktop, in the corner where the two counters meet. In this way, B. is remarkable. She leans when she walks and her fingers are like sticks. Her T-shirt has a stain on it. And yet there she is, on the counter, feet kicking. Girlish.

"I went out this morning and Dog, he's gone." Flo is repeating herself, she cannot help it. "And I heard from Teddy. There was a card. She wrote me a note."

"That's how she shows her love." B. knows about Teddy. "Quite a day," she adds. "Quite a day, huh? Oh honey. Honey pie. There are days, aren't there? With our kids."

Flo knows that by kids, B. means Dog, too. To B., animals are also our children. B. herself once had a human child, a son who was deaf. "Bear wasn't lonely," B. will sometimes say with satisfaction. His given name was Brian, but always, to B., he was Bear. Bear died of a rare form of cancer years ago, but B. says she keeps him close by remembering. Now, legs still kicking, she tells Flo about the time they were staying at a cabin in the Tetons and a bad storm was coming. Bear was a child, not even ten. It was just B. and Bear, the way it was, once, just Flo and Teddy.

Flo hasn't heard this story before.

"It was dark," B. says. "We lost power and I didn't know where he was." She picks up the mug with its muffin inside, rolling the mug between her hands and shaking her head, remembering. "I started calling out for him." B. laughs. "He couldn't hear me, of course! But what else could I do? I was shouting—screaming, really—into the wind. And I thought: my son has never heard his name."

B. keeps green onions in a glass of water on the counter, snipping the fresh shoots for cooking. They grow back, again and again. They are tireless, and Flo admires them.

"Then he came from behind the barn they had at that place," B. says. "I forgot about everything else and we went inside and watched the storm together."

Flo smooths her skirt with her hands. Bear died before his life got strange, or nasty; there is no way to explain to B. the possible luck in that. In death Bear remains special to his mother. He remains intact. While Flo sometimes wonders if—no, she suspects—Teddy isn't so special after all.

Sucking at her teeth, she gazes at the onions, which seem to have adapted to their life in an unexpected, unnatural place.

Teddy wasn't so special but she also was, being Teddy. The same could be said of Flo herself, of course.

"Teddy says it's time for the two of us to do something together," she says abruptly. "Or something like that. In her letter. That's a good thing. Right?" Flo trusts B.

"We spend time with the ones we love," B. agrees.

"Maybe I didn't spend enough time with that dog and he quit me." Flo whispers this, but B. hears her anyway. That B.! She doesn't miss a trick.

"Dog knows he's loved. He's a good judge of character. He'll be back."

"I wish animals could talk," Flo says.

"They do."

B. says these things and, truly, she believes what she says. B. carries her belief like fire in a horn.

Flo is drawn to B.'s belief, she is consoled by it. It was the same with Sunby, of course. They both remind her of what might be possible, of goodness.

She used to think she was good, or good enough. She used to think her daughter was good enough, too.

3

There once was a woman with three daughters, and they were all good-enough girls. This was during a time when cats chewed tobacco and monkeys used cutlery—this was not your time, nor was it mine. But for the woman and her daughters, it was the present.

The girls' father had died when they were very young. They never knew him, not really, and they were used to being without him; it therefore felt natural that it fell to their mother to work hard, to give them a place in the world. That was the way of things. The family lived in a tiny wooden house on the side of a mountain, the good soil there as red as puppy drum. As they grew to womanhood each daughter said, in turn, that they wanted to see the world. Let's see who I meet, each said. Let's see where the world takes me.

4

FLO REMEMBERS the stories her mother told her. She used to share them with Teddy; she shares them with B. now. The storytelling began after Flo, four years old, had to have surgery to correct a wandering eye. Before the surgery Flo saw double, and assumed everyone did. She was a little surprised, maybe even disappointed, when she understood that this was not the case.

Seeing just one of everything after surgery—the world seemed less substantial, somehow. And Flo hated the eyedrops that helped her eye heal.

She had to lie down. There was the drip. Then a blink. Blink blink.

Ugh! Flo would cry and squirm, day after day; looking back, it is hard to understand why the drops were such an ordeal. But maybe that was the beginning, a glint of knowing that nothing was certain. Her mother, who meant well, would say we didn't want to turn blind, did we? Let's fix this.

So. There was that.

In any case Flo cried, and the promise was that she would hear a story only if she would lie still. "No drops, no story," Flo's mother, also named Flo, always said. She was pragmatic. Also, a fatalist. It was the Slavic in her. These are popular myths, Flo's mother said about the stories she told, though later, much later, Flo looked these characters up and she could not find them.

Maybe they were old Czech tales, translated and related so many times that they had become unrecognizable, even to the teller. Flo the younger was second-generation, born in this country; her maternal grandfather was the only person she knew who spoke Czech. When he did, it was like a party trick, much like the way he would, when she was a child, make her laugh by removing his upper plate after dinner. It lounged on his tongue, a yellow grin, until he snapped it back into place.

"Everything has an end except for a sausage, which has two." Or at least that's what he said he said, in Czech, and Flo would dutifully smile. She must have been eight. What did she know about endings? When he gave her a Czech/English dictionary, she never cracked it, though out of a certain nostalgia, or reverence, it has followed her everywhere since.

Later, when she became a teen, her grandfather didn't understand her. Or perhaps he understood her too well. By 15 she had thickened—her waist, her hips—and she was always on one diet or another. She thought her white painter pants made her ass look big. She drank cup after cup of black coffee, and her grandfather would stare. "You just like coffee because there are no calories," he said, his voice not quite scornful.

How did he know this? Flo, her stomach roiling with caffeine, could not imagine. She hated that he found her vapid, but she could not say that he misread her. She started drinking tea after that. Everything has an end, she was beginning to understand.

When Flo tells her mother's stories they are not quite the same—how could they be?—but she tries to stick the landing, she tries to get the endings right. And the stories, they help her feel grounded. They make Flo feel close to what she once was: a mother herself.

5

FLO FEELS TIRED, thinking about Teddy's letter. More tired than the heat makes her; this is a weariness no amount of sleep can cure. "I haven't read the whole letter yet," she admits to B. There is no way to explain what she doesn't understand herself: that she is afraid of what Teddy might have to say. She shrugs, instead. "Lemme take a quick look outside; I bet Dog is back."

B. nods and unlocks her front door that was a back door, once; she waits while Flo circles the house. Flo shakes her head when she returns; the feeling of Dog is lesser now, somehow.

"No sign of him. SilverGirl will be beside herself." Because Dog and SilverGirl are bonded; they sleep draped over one another, snoring quietly. They share the stuffed toy shaped like a smiling pizza.

B. nods. "SilverGirl will be upset if Dog is lost," she says. "I know you will, too."

"How am I going to find him?" Flo's voice holds hope in it, and also a lack of hope.

B. embraces Flo, then lets go. Her body is as bent as it was before. Flo feels a rush of affection so intense that tears sting her eyes, and B.'s face is kind when she says, "Perhaps he'll find you."

6

The eldest daughter was named Severina—though maybe, because so much time has passed, today she would be a Sally. She was tall and proud, and her gift (or curse) was her honesty; she would never cheat another, knowingly. She also spoke the truth, all of it. When it came time for her adventure, her mother packed her off with:

- *A sliver of soap.*
- *A biscuit.*
- *A bottle of beer.*

On Severina's first day out in the world, she came upon an old man by a stile. He asked for food and so Severina gave him a pinch of her biscuit. The old fellow ate the biscuit in one bite—he was that hungry. He thanked her graciously. Then he said, "Tell me, daughter, do you think I am handsome?"

Now, the old man was so old that his skin was pebbled, like a lizard's. His eyes were canny and his head as bald as an egg. He was a wizard, surely.

"You are ugly," Severina said without hesitation. "And you smell." She pulled the slip of soap from her pocket and gave it to him.

"You speak truly," the man shrugged. "And I thank you for the soap." Then he told her to walk for three days, hard north, and that if she did, on the third day she would find her husband.

And so the girl did, walking confidently over fields and hills, fording streams, until she got to a high dry field. There she found a house made entirely of nickel, with a nice deep porch that ran three sides around. It shone dully in the wintry sun of that place, and there were cattle grazing before it the same color as the house.

Severina waded through the cattle, who huffed and chewed, but before she reached the steps of the porch, a tall man came out the front door. He called to her by name, and before day's end they were married and had sent good tidings and casks of cream back to the house on the red mountain.

The tall man was Severina's rightful partner, and the two lived happily enough. The old wizard, grateful for the biscuit (and, to a lesser degree, the soap), had made certain that they met. But he was proud and vain in his way, and Severina's comments stung. In the end, he kept back from the girl certain gifts: the ability to speak with animals, for example. And so, though the cattle gave of their milk freely, they never loved her as they might have. They never said a word.

7

SUNBY ALWAYS SAID he appreciated Teddy's honesty.

Sunby, who will be "laid to rest" in Ephrem. Flo knows the cemetery, with its LED solar crosses and plastic flowers. Mrs. Benedict is buried there. Flo didn't attend Mrs. Benedict's service (she wasn't invited), which was packed, she heard. Many people will be at Sunby's service also: he was a pastor, and beloved. Not Flo's pastor—she's never been a churchgoer—but he was Flo's friend. And a good one. She tries to imagine going to his funeral and she would like to, for Nell, Sunby's widow, but the costs of travel are prohibitive, for one thing, and for another, now Teddy is coming.

One thing at a time, Flo thinks.

Besides. She knows she would be the extra one, and there will be a coldness there, not from Nell but from the others. Or, worse, a curiosity: about herself, about Teddy. When it doesn't have to do with them, people love to be frightened.

Sunby died of cancer, but Mrs. Benedict died from a blow to the head. During the long weeks of the trial, Flo forced herself to understand the mechanics of what had happened to the teacher. A brain being like jelly on a plate, she read. How if you shake the plate the jelly will shake, it will tear. The brain can swell, and if it does it might squeeze shut the arteries, the blood vessels that supply it with blood.

Never ignore a blow to the head, the articles said. Flo learned about coup injuries, contrecoup injuries, the names putting her in mind of dictatorships, of military juntas. She tried to stop reading but . . .

Well.

A person whose brain is not receiving fresh blood will lose consciousness. It doesn't take long. Eight to 10 seconds, Flo read. Without the oxygen, without fresh blood, the brain begins to die. This takes four to six minutes. Flo still doesn't know how long it took for Mrs. Benedict to die. She was dead when her husband found her. Teddy had run away through the field, her footprints tiny in the vast stretch of mud and snow.

"It was an accident, Mama," Teddy said, and her voice was still green, it hadn't darkened yet. Teddy might have said something else, too, about standing up for their little family. The family Flo had made.

What sticks with Flo is this: Teddy, at 14, had not called her Mama for so long. And in the years since? No "Mamas" at all, not a one.

Bad things happen, Flo understands, and sometimes there is no fixing them. It was humbling to think how jolly she'd been, although if you'd asked her back then she would have said she had her worries. She had been happy, she realized only when the happiness ended. She'd taken it for granted. Of course.

After Flo leaves B., she stands in her own kitchen and reassures the cats, who have clustered around her again. "I've got this," she tells them. "And when we are all back together we'll travel through the blue door. You, and me, and Dog."

The cats contemplate her, satisfied; Flo nods at each of them in turn. She pulls Teddy's card from her pocket. "You should know," the next lines say. "You should know that I have been on a journey."

Also: "I've been lonely," Teddy says.

Flo scratches at her neck. "Maybe Teddy can come too? Through the blue door?" she asks the cats. But they are inscrutable, they will not say.

Sunby once observed that in the aftermath of trauma, one response is to try to control what we can. Controlling the narrative, he called it. They were talking on the phone, they were back in touch. Because there was a period of time during which no one knew where Flo had gone, she'd left the house in Ephrem and gone to JuvieLand and she hadn't even told Sunby, she hadn't told Nell. Her move to be close to Teddy being no one's business. After a time Flo called Sunby, though, and told him where she had settled. He was her friend, after all.

And Sunby liked Teddy. Teddy liked Sunby. Though Flo had met him first—he and Nell took Flo under their wing in the aftermath of the trial—he began visiting Teddy in the facility for juveniles, and he did so for all the years she was there. Even though it was a haul. A full day for the visit, the drive downstate and back—even when he didn't know Flo had followed Teddy to that town. Especially then, perhaps.

Sunby was reassuringly kind when she called, acting as though they had spoken just the day before. Though in fact it had been months since they last met, at a restaurant in the mall back in Ephrem. It was pure friendship they shared, nothing more, though the locals speculated about that, too. Flo could have told them: Sunby watched out for the underdog, the misunderstood. Flo fit the bill.

At the restaurant, Sunby had ordered cookies with gritty frosting so thick it was as though it had been applied with a trowel. So over the top, those cookies were, though Flo had wanted hers anyway. With great effort she had not eaten it; Flo's lawyer had warned her to be careful, not to eat anything in public or at least not anything that had left her sight. Sunby wouldn't have done anything to the cookies, of course, but maybe their waitress, an older woman who smiled at Sunby but not Flo, could have.

Flo called Sunby from downstate because she needed someone besides Teddy to know where she lived, that she lived. By telling Sunby she became less invisible and her new life became real. Flo visited Teddy, and Sunby and sometimes Nell visited Teddy. They were like Pando, the giant aspen: one great organism, all the trunks linked. That's what Sunby said.

She never lost touch with Sunby again after that (until his death, of course). She does not know Nell nearly as well, although they are closer in age, and certainly friendly.

But really, in Flo's eyes, it was always the three of them: Sunby, and Teddy, and Flo.

"What's going to happen?" Flo asked Sunby after Teddy did what she did. After the police found Teddy crouched in the woods, her jeans brown with the teacher's blood. (If Mrs. Benedict's brain was not receiving blood, where did all the blood come from? Flo doesn't know.)

Three times Flo asked Sunby, "What's going to happen?" Because although Sunby and Nell tried to shield her, Flo still heard the gossip. How the woods were silent that day—not even the birds could bring themselves to sing, the locals said—and that Teddy herself was like a beast when they tracked her down. Or feral. Someone said.

The story had grown to claim them both: Flo wasn't stupid, she knew what the Ephrem people thought of her. "I still believe in myself," she lied. And Sunby, who knew better, said nothing—he extended to her that kindness.

Flo reaches down to pet SilverGirl and the slim narrow cat called Minnow, who reminds Flo of Teddy. A little. Flo thinks she should take off work for Teddy's visit. She also thinks she should keep everything the same.

It is easier to think about Dog. His paws like a yeti. That's what B. always said, anyway.

If Flo went to Sunby's funeral, her feet would be pink and swollen, trapped like pigeons in her "good" sandals with their tight gilded straps. Flo has only worn them once. Once was enough. She likes her red shoes. But you cannot wear red shoes to a funeral: Flo hears her own mother's voice in her head, instructing her.

The fact is that with Sunby gone, there is no reason to go to Ephrem again. Without him, it is just a memory of a town. Like a ruin, with its dying mall. Its community college and Walmart and humdrum cemetery. This is how Flo remembers it.

Sunby never got to form an impression of where Flo lives now. He and Nell had planned to visit, later this year, when winter came to Illinois. "Snowbirds come here," Flo had told them on the phone. They could visit the old prison, she said, and Sunby seemed tickled by the thought of a photo of him there, under the archway. His feet would have been flat and wide in their sandals. Like paws they would have been.

They would have broken bread together.

Flo slips the card back into her pocket. It is already getting creased. Soon it will be like most of the other notes from Teddy, soft from wear.

She steps outside. Dog, she thinks. The Place has come into her mind. She calls it The Place, as the dog is Dog; it is just a patch of ground with a stripe of water. Flo likes the idea of water, which seems hopeful, existing as it does even here, in the desert.

She found The Place one day when she was out walking; now she returns, again and again. She returns because she senses The Place holds within it something she needs; there is the solace of nature, certainly, but also something else, something she can't pinpoint. Not yet. Often she brings Dog and it is a good walk for them both. It is their walk, and when they arrive, some things are always the same. The bank is banded with pointy rocks, for example. But the river has its seasons, its different faces. It has been a freshet, a broad ribbon. It has been a filthy green seepage.

Perhaps Dog will be there. He knows The Place; surely he'd go there first. That is where she will look for him. Also she needs to get on with things: buy groceries for her daughter, and wash the extra set of sheets, which Flo will tuck around the couch cushions. Teddy said she is coming soon.

Soon. Now. So much. Like an itch you can't scratch. Flo used to think that she knew how to do this—be there for others.

She cracks her back and looks up. It's a Jell-O sky, cloudy yellow, and the air is still cool enough. Flo is glad for her sweatshirt, though later it will be too much.

The animals are fed (they eat high-protein food). B. is fed (she eats all that is sweet).

Flo starts walking.

8

Today Flo walks to find Dog.

The act, the walking itself, is familiar and thus reassuring. Because every day holds these things: First tea, the animals. B. Then walking. The walks: they are epic and a part of her life now. Flo can hardly remember a time when they weren't.

But the walking really started when Flo lived in Ephrem, after Teddy was sent away. At the time Flo, who had started to neglect her work at the community college, took long lunches. She walked through those lunches, eating her sandwich on the move, and this on the days she remembered to eat at all.

There was a pond at the college. Flo walked around and around it, she walked the surrounding subdivisions, though she avoided the neighborhood where Mrs. Benedict had lived. When the weather was foul, she crossed Cardinal Highway and walked the indoor mall. Movement being an almost sacred act. An expression of survival that has been known since ancient times (Flo thinks).

And time moved differently on those walks, so slowly and steadily that her concerns almost became beside the point; she walked to forget herself. To forget Teddy and the diagnoses that proliferated and seemed, to Flo, to contradict one another: Paranoia, one doctor said. Narcissism, another insisted. Attachment anxiety. When Teddy was eventually released from Juvie, no one used the word "cured"; Flo has never asked her daughter if she is on medication ("Don't ask the question you don't want the answer to," Flo's mother used to say).

Sometimes Flo still walks to forget. But today? Today she walks to find Dog.

He was agreeable, Flo thinks. He *is* agreeable, she corrects herself.

Surely not everything ends badly.

9

The second sister was short and wide, with a merry freckled face. Her name was Hilaria. Hilaria kept her hair in two plaits, and it was both her gift and her curse that she took nothing very seriously. She was not one to fret or plan, but eventually, some months after Severina's wedding, Hilaria decided that it was time to go out into the world also. "Let's see what I find, Mother," she said, and the girls' mother sent her off with:

- *Charcoal powder.*

and, because she was the sweetest of the three girls:

- *A wedge of cake.*
- *A flask of cherry wine.*

Before too much time had passed, Hilaria came upon the same old man, waiting by the stile. He said he was thirsty and so she gave him her wine to drink. The wizard thanked her, then asked the same question he had asked her sister. "Am I handsome?" he said, preening a little.

The wizard was still ugly—enough time had passed that he might have been even a little uglier—but Hilaria responded carelessly, hardly looking before responding, "Of course, Father, you are the handsomest man I know."

Now the wizard knew the girl was lying, but he also recognized her kindness (she'd given him most of her wine), and so he told her to walk three days to the south, and that if she did, on the third day she would find her husband. Hilaria did so, though at a slower pace than her tall and determined elder sister. On the third day, in a low green valley, Hilaria came upon a house made entirely of copper, with a cupola on the top and a small flock of sheep graz-

ing before it. She had no sooner stepped onto the path leading up to the house than a round man with a cheerful face leaned out of the cupola and called her by name. Before the sun had dropped behind the valley that day, he and Hilaria were married, and they sent their tidings and cakes of the softest wool yarn back to Hilaria's red mountain home.

Of course the cheerful-faced man was Hilaria's rightful partner, and the two lived happily enough. But the old wizard, who knew Hilaria had not responded seriously to his question, kept back from her certain gifts: the ability to spin yarn, for example. And though the wool produced by their sheep was the finest in the land, and the couple made a good living from it, only Hilaria's husband could prepare the yarn. And so it was that Hilaria and her husband were always two steps behind, a little breathless, as they made their way through the world.

10

Teddy was never particularly cheerful, even as a baby, but Flo, who for so many years accepted what made Teddy different, thought that so long as her daughter experienced joy, even a quiet joy, she (Flo) would be satisfied. And when Teddy was little, Flo was pretty sure that Teddy did experience joy. She did!

"I am your blind spot," Teddy had written in one of her recent, shorter cards. This was pretty much all the card said. There was a heron on the front of that one. Flo thought what Teddy said was probably true, but still, the observation hurt. She usually saves mail from Teddy but this card she threw away. She threw it away at work so she wouldn't be tempted to dig it out later. The card lay on someone else's discarded lunch, and Flo dumped her own almost-full cup of coffee over it all. Just to be sure. The scene is freakishly clear in her mind: the soggy heron, even the skirt Flo wore that day, with its soft rose-colored plaid.

Today Flo is wearing that same skirt, it's her favorite. Such a good shade of pink! She is wearing her oversized sweatshirt, also pink, but neon, with a puffy design on the front. A bear. Flo knows it is a sweatshirt for an old lady, or a small child, but she is right between these, isn't she? A middle age. Under the sweatshirt that is almost (but not quite) absurd is a T-shirt with a hole in it, and a fanny pack is slung around her hips. Fanny packs: they are in fashion again, apparently. Flo has seen kids in the store recently, wearing them like bandoliers, although Flo has used this one for decades. It's pink also.

"Pink is your color," Teddy said once. Pink was also the color of the frosting on the store-bought cakes they ate together. These cakes came nestled in pristine boxes of midwinter white and were good enough, if achingly sweet; Teddy and Flo could happily plow through one in a couple days' time.

Once though, for special, Flo made a cake entirely from scratch. She meant to delight Teddy and she did. "Flo!" Teddy said. "This is a good cake." "You like him?" Flo asked, and they were both pleased, eating the cake with their fingers and it was still warm.

The sun beats down, but Flo has always run cold, even when she weighed more, even when she took up more space. Flo looks at her neighbor's house as she passes. He is an older man, his skin thick as shoes. He is not out as he sometimes is, smoking a cigarette, and Flo is sorry. He has the kindness in him.

Maybe in another lifetime they will be friends, Flo thinks.

Flo imagines these alternative versions of her life, usually at night. Nights can be hard. B. goes to bed early. There is no one to tell Flo stories. There is no one to tell stories to. Well, there are the animals, and so Flo tells them about a blue door. This door is hard to find, Flo says. It's painted a most appealing blue. Blue as a damselfly, she says, and it leads to an alternate life, another life for all of them. All the animals are there! (She wouldn't tell them about it if they weren't.)

She used to tell Teddy about the blue door. Also.

"Dog!" Flo calls half-heartedly. She sits on the curb. She pulls out Teddy's card again.

"I wish I had a blue door," Teddy writes. Flo closes the card. She closes her eyes. She wonders what would lie beyond Teddy's door, what alternate life a young woman like Teddy might yearn for. Perhaps one in which love was not so appallingly violent?

For starters.

Flo sometimes feels as though she has lived many lives. One time, in another life, a more substantial Flo stayed with Teddy at a hotel in Wisconsin. It was a special place, made to look like a lodge, and there were friendly carved bears everywhere a person might look. Flo bought Teddy the oversized pink sweatshirt with the bear on it. Somehow it looked right on Teddy, who has always been so pale and ethereal, although this garment is one of the things Teddy has left behind.

Flo likes sweatshirts: to give, and to wear.

There was a pool at the hotel, and even though it was Wisconsin, and winter, the pool was indoors but also outdoors. You could swim through a channel, under plastic flags, and emerge in the pool outside, which despite the time of year was not as cold as you might think. Even Flo, who hated the cold, would swim out there for short periods of time. Steam rose off the water, which mirrored in its depths the silver sky. The climbing ladder in the outdoor pool wore a thin skin of ice, but when you swam back inside, the indoor pool room—painted with bears and eagles and pines—was humid and warm as a jungle. Like a miracle.

Mornings they rose early and swam before anyone else thought to show up with their swim noodles and goggles. Flo wore a pink swimsuit with a racer back.

Once upon a time her cup had something in it, Flo thinks. They were happy. Or Flo was, in any case. Because there was no one Flo wanted to be with then, more than Teddy. She wasn't lonely in their family of two, she was exactly where she wanted to be. And Flo, who believed then that she was doing it right—being a mother, being *Teddy's* mother—thought hell yeah. Yes. I'm someone good.

11

The girls' mother thought she knew exactly what she had taken on, having all these children. Each one being so different. This is what she had learned:

- *The first required strength.*
- *The second required patience.*
- *And oh gods, the third . . .*

12

After what Teddy did, Flo realized that she was a stranger not only to her daughter but to herself. She was astonished. Astonished! This is still so, and the effort to understand them both might be her only chance at grace.

Sunby once said that astonishment and grace are connected. He rarely invoked the Bible when he and Flo talked—he knew how she felt about it—but just the once, in the aftermath of Mrs. Benedict's death, he talked about that confluence of astonishment and grace as he understood it. "That's what it means to be thunderstruck," he said, adding that the multitudes in the Bible were thunderstruck.

Flo wants to be thunderstruck. She burns to know—herself, her child.

For now, though. Flo pushes up from the curb and tells herself that she will have to be satisfied with:

- Keeping moving.
- Not scratching unless she can help it.
- At least until she finds Dog.

And Dog is nowhere to be found, and the burning is literal, Flo's eczema with its cratered edges. She has developed eczema, she doesn't know why she gets it where she does: her elbows, her hands. Even inside her ears! Right now virulent patches simmer on her shoulders and neck. For most of her life, Flo never had skin problems. Then the Benedict woman died and it was like Flo changed skins entirely.

Well. The dermatologist said that people change, our bodies change. He said it like an after-school special. Or the filmstrips Flo had to watch in health class, once upon a time.

Usually Flo scratches at the rash lightly—which nevertheless raises the tiny bumps, beaks of heat like little mouths—then harder, raking with her strong nails which are her last vestige of youth. Sometimes she has drawn blood but other times there is just a clear seeping. Today the patches are raw.

But she walks resolutely, red shoes clacking—act the way you want to feel, she used to tell Teddy. Dog will be at The Place, Flo tells herself. He will be resting by the river. Flo imagines him there, she can almost see it!

Ugh. Eczema. Flo scrapes at it with her nails. The steroid cream Flo uses gives her skin a waxy feel but it also provides some relief. Sometimes it does. The cream must be used sparingly: too much and the skin gets thin, the doctor warned. Flo tries to be disciplined about this. She tries to have a good attitude about the lozenges of raised flesh. As Flo's own mother used to say, it could all be so much worse. (Could it? *Oh yes*, Flo assures herself grimly. It could be. It has been.)

Every day Flo misses her mother, who was very much her own person but still knew how to be in the world. Flo admires this. She herself is weird, getting weirder, probably.

And Teddy! Well.

13

There was good and evil in this world. There was no way to anticipate it all.

14

"HELLO!" SHE SAYS emphatically to a man on his porch. He lives several blocks over, his house immaculate. His forehead, broad and knobby, is red from the sun. He keeps a dog with one cloudy eye.

One time the cloud eye lunged at Flo and Dog when they walked by. They were on their way to The Place; the man said Dog should be on a leash. Or a chain. Dog forgave Cloud Eye immediately; Flo knows this, it is his nature. Flo has likewise tried to forgive the man's dog. She has tried to forgive the man, for his unkindness. This is not easy for her. She can hold a grudge.

Because: what else did he say? She shouldn't have a dog. She should get rid of him, Dog didn't belong to her.

"Well, he belongs to himself," Flo had said with what she hoped was dignity. And she believed this. She didn't think one creature should belong to another. She also believed that as affable as Dog was in general, what they shared, she and Dog, was unique.

Now every day Flo passes here she greets them both, man and his dog. She finds the man strange, but she is trying to be a better person, an effort that started in JuvieLand and hasn't stopped, not yet. Some day she will ask the man his name, she will ask the name of the cloud eye; this is important because Flo knows that names are important. She knows this from the stories her mother told.

"Good morning!" she screams out. The cloud eye, lounging on the porch with his man, startles, and Flo takes a breath, then continues more quietly. "Have you seen my dog? He's about this high? Reddish fur?" The man stares. "I . . .

I don't know the breed. But he's a very good dog." On this point Flo is certain. "*My* dog," she repeats. But the cloud eye just sneers, the man looks past her.

"That's not your dog. If it ever was." Did the man just say this? Surely not. Now he's looking at her and he's smiling but not exactly.

He said *something* anyway, fast and monotone, and despite everything, it occurs to Flo that the man might help her find Dog. The thought cracks her world just that little bit more open. Flo feels a sense of possibility. Hope, even.

"If you see him, can you . . . call this number?" Moving closer, Flo unzips her fanny pack and rifles through it. There is a golf pencil, there is an old receipt. She scrawls her number on the back of the receipt. "Maybe hold onto him until I can come get him?"

"I'll hold onto him," the man says. He's come off the porch and accepts the paper, folding it and slipping it into the pocket of his cargo shorts. "But I keep on telling you."

She doesn't understand half of what he is saying, but she reaches out to shake his hand anyway. The man's hand is dry and small; she feels the bones in it.

"I don't know you," she admits. "I'm Flo."

"Oh I know who you are," he says. "You walk to the river, you drag that dog around in the heat. No leash. No chain."

"He is very well behaved," Flo says, pulling her hand away. "I want him to be free."

(Teddy was free now, wasn't she? Flo thinks this, she hopes.)

"Freedom!" The man pauses and spits to the side. "Overrated," he declares. The man's forehead is positively lumpy, and Flo tries not to stare at it. "Lemme show you something," the man says. "Lemme show you something real." He's pointing into his side yard, where there is a small shelter for the cloud eye. A pan of water. On the side of the shelter is written, SAFE FROM THE BASTARDS, in painted letters that have run so that each letter has its own wormy legs.

Flo surprises herself by laughing. "I like that!" It's a delighted laugh—one of Flo's pet phrases is *don't let the bastards get you down*—and in that moment the man seems pleased. But then he frowns.

"I let him run, he's not safe. And I get what I deserve. You see?" He stabs his finger at her. "We reap what we sow." He eyes her up and down, her red plastic shoes, the sweatshirt meant for a child. "Free!" he scoffs.

Flo shifts from one foot to another, the moment between them having passed. "You don't know me," she says finally. "You don't know Dog."

"I know you," he says. "And remember what I told you," he adds. "About the dog. Remember." The man's near-grin appears again, an afterthought. "You need a chain, you need a rope. You need to take *accountability*."

"Well," Flo says. "Anyway. In case you find him." She pauses, then: "What's your name?" She is asking. Finally.

"None of your business," the man says, and he turns away. Cloud Eye turns too, lip curled.

Flo resumes walking and now she walks angrily; she doesn't look back. She tries not to scratch at her neck. What a weirdo! She wishes she hadn't given him her number.

The effort it all takes: managing her skin, talking to people. Being *discerning*. She keeps herself clean, but she has calluses on her feet, hard and glittering from all the walking. Her T-shirt has the hole to be mended—her skin window, Flo calls it—and the sparkly red shoes are scuffed, their heels ground down. She tells herself now that the man with his cloudy-eyed dog would judge her no matter how she looked. There is never adequate time to fix it all.

But it's always been this way. One time, in the house Flo and Charlie briefly owned, the sewer line backed up and there was a mess of gray water. They peeled up the ruined carpet squares in the family room and tried to clean the bare floor with dish soap. There wasn't money to replace the carpet.

Flo gave herself a day to cry over her ruined things. Then she arranged the couch in front of the television. She wore thick socks against the ugliness of exposed laminate, which was scarred and dull. Lifting her chin, she refused to look down at it. Instead she hummed, holding little Teddy close; her determination to overcome disappointment was a hard kernel in her gut.

Charlie, who in Flo's opinion didn't have as much going on—in life, in his head—might have been making tuna casserole for dinner. He might have been out drinking with his one friend. Charlie drank too much; he lacked ambition. Flo, who wanted to go back to school, was starting to think of herself as cut from a different cloth.

But Teddy still mattered; she was everything. Together, Flo and her daughter, they looked at the TV. Was it a comfort? It was, and something they were to do together, for years and years until news of Teddy reached the screen. At that point television became markedly less fun, a reminder of all that had been lost. After Teddy was sent away there was a period when Flo stopped watching altogether. Then Silver-Girl came into her life, and Flo finally had someone to watch with again.

15

THE BLOCKS THAT SURROUND the house where Flo lives now are blasted with light. The homes here aren't built for lifetimes; they might not even last one, well-lived. Flo's neighborhood is humble, and this humility suited her when she came upon it and decided to settle. That was some three years ago now, Flo's car engine banging so alarmingly that the decision to stay put was made for her.

Plus there was something reassuring about this town. It had been home to the Pied Piper, once upon a time. A *serial killer*, but the town had survived. And there was this: someone here had done things far worse than Teddy had ever done.

Now Flo passes low residences painted in sensible light colors, fronted with gravel instead of grass, or sometimes bare dirt, which she still cannot reconcile herself to. But this is no place for grass: one season only and it dries to straw. Acacias grow in some of the yards, and do well enough. There is one angry-looking desert willow she passes every day. Flo tries not to look at it, its unhappiness being catching and Flo herself so susceptible. In one yard, there is gravel glued down and painted green.

Flo passes between two adobe pillars that mark the neighborhood: Cactus Glen! the pillars proclaim. She turns onto a sidewalk that follows the four-lane *stroad* like an afterthought; now there are a few churches, the big-box kind, the ones that stayed open for in-person services even during COVID, or through most of it, anyway. Flo wasn't here yet when the pandemic hit, she was still in JuvieLand, but she's heard from B. about how things were. Most of the churches have a little food pantry out front: cabinets with glass-front doors, always set on a post and sometimes fitted with a shingled roof. Before COVID these structures held books for sharing, B. said, and during COVID they held nonperishables. They still do. "Leave something if you can, take what you need," the signs say. Flo sometimes gets her peanut butter here. If there is ever rice, Flo takes it, for mixing into the animals' food. One outstanding day there were two packets of the jam cookies B. likes, and Flo took them both to surprise her friend. B. *was* surprised, and happy, though the cookies were only there the once.

Flo pauses at the improvised food pantry in front of a church that has the square windowless dimensions of a mausoleum. She's hungry. Flo made the muffin for B. but forgot to eat anything herself. Just that bit of pear. This particular little library/food pantry is shaped like a church (of course). It even has a steeple. Flo moves closer, peers through the glass. Today there are:

- One bag of flour.
- A jar of olives.
- A loaf of bread.

The bread looks dense and thick with seeds! Flo opens the pantry door. She extracts the bread and eats three slices, one plus one plus one, right where she stands. Then she twists the tie on the bread bag and returns the loaf to the pantry. She has taken what she needs. She can continue her walk: into the day, to Dog, past the other churches.

The largest churches look like malls. And if they are ugly, Sunby might say, what of it? (Sunby! How can it be that she will never talk with him again?) His church in Ephrem had been a storefront. Flo never once attended his services and he never held this against her. He always laughed and said Flo ministered to *him*.

Here are two more churches in a row. Safety in numbers. At Christmas every one of them has a nativity scene out front. You can tell if the church is struggling by whether the nativity figures are hollow molded plastic as opposed to concrete or painted wood.

At one church in particular, the plastic figures are exceptionally cheap, flimsy and lightweight so that they would be easy to steal. Last year it even crossed Flo's mind: *Take what you need*. At the time she thought, maybe I need a plastic Jesus. But then she decided that she doesn't have any interest in the Baby Jesus, accomplished as he must have been; though Sunby always spoke so glowingly of Christ, Flo has soured on little children. One of the animals might be nice, though. Flo thinks this now, although it's April, the nativity figures burrowed away in some hallowed corner until the season arrives again. Flo remembers the plastic molded donkey that the church puts out every year; he has a winning look to him. His face being like Dog's, sincere.

(Dog's face: Flo can see it so clearly in her mind's eye! She feels within herself a knife of anxiety; she is picturing coyotes again, the way they can work together in packs to kill their prey.)

"Dog!" Flo walks more quickly now, passing strip malls that are not churches. Obviously. (Though, and Flo thinks this is a fair point, they are churches of consumerism. Right? Sunby would get a chuckle out of *that* one, wouldn't he!) The stores are still veiled, cool and dark, at this hour. Some of them stay shuttered all day. Some businesses closed here, as they did everywhere, during COVID. Not every space has been filled with something new.

It's not a lovely town but it possesses an unsentimental quality that Teddy may like. It's warm all year 'round, for one thing. Once Flo tried to fry an egg on the sidewalk outside her apartment, to prove to herself how hot it gets. She had just moved here when she did this; the differences of this place were still a wonder. A passerby watched, disapproving, at the mess Flo made, so she abandoned her efforts. For weeks after, there was a stain on the concrete where the egg had been.

When they lived in Ephrem, Teddy was always cold. Like her mother! But unlike Flo, Teddy never complained; she'd told her mother once that complaining just made it worse, so why bother? And Teddy suffered from chilblains, as if she were trapped in an earlier century. Her lips would turn blue. The one winter they lived there together, Flo remembers, was so long that the icicles growing from the eaves of their house were as thick and long as a man's arm. One time she and Teddy threw snowballs at them until a few fell into the drifts banked against the house. There had probably been a few minutes of light left when they brought the icicles inside, sucking at them like freezer pops. Pretending that they were banana flavored. Teddy held hers to her head; she was pretending to be a unicorn. Or a narwhal, Flo said. She said this, or some of it at least, in their own language of Derrykin. She didn't know the Derrykin for narwhal, though.

The lilt of that name! Derrykin. Flo thought it sounded cheerful, something special, happy, that just the two of them shared. Teddy had come up with the language, but Flo had invented its name at Teddy's insistence. The language itself seemed somehow strangely familiar, as though Flo had spoken it in another life (beyond the blue door?). Or in a dream.

There are no vowels in Derrykin. There are symbols, certainly, with their own weird sounds. Their own rich nature. One wavers like a theremin. Another is reminiscent of the strident call of the cranes Teddy knew Flo loved.

Teddy remembers Derrykin, but she seems to recall little else about the childhood Flo tried to create for her. "I don't remember any of it," Teddy told her once. Her voice pitiless, almost reckless; she was still in Juvie, then. Flo doesn't know what to make of this. It worries her; she understands that memories are a part of who we are.

For instance, the afternoon of the icicles, in the stinging warmth of the Ephrem kitchen, their faces flushed the chopped red of strawberries. The dying day pressed against the fogged kitchen window, which was never very clean. And there was the sound of yipping; Ephrem suffered from a plague of foxes. Flo remembers this. They were always yipping.

The way Flo recalls it, the rising darkness was fleecy through the dirty windows. The cries of the foxes only underlined how safe Flo and Teddy were, and Flo squeezed her daughter in a side-arm hug; Teddy still let her do that, then. She was 14. Things were already changing between them but sometimes, when they were alone, the hugs were still—Flo wants to think they were still—welcome. And real.

That was a perfect day. Even in Ephrem. How could Teddy not remember this? How could Teddy not remember how it was, the two of them, once upon a time?

16

Flo stops and slips the card out of her pocket again; this card, it burns, like or worse than the eczema. Like the sting of those cholla cactus spines when she has accidentally knocked a hand against them. Why does it burn? Because.

Because the card is this: it's Teddy coming to visit, but it's also Flo, something to do with who she, Flo, is, or has been, or might have been.

Who she has become.

She opens the card and skips past the lines she's already read. "I've been north," Teddy says. "I've been west. It's time for me to go deeper. I might be south soon enough, by ____, I reckon." Teddy has written a date and underlined it. The date being not so far away. "I'm coming," Teddy says a second time.

Flo closes her eyes. She can see Teddy's face clearly, cool and remote. Her hair white-blond, for it never dimmed or yellowed; it has remained, always, as bright as hay. Flo remembers suddenly the way her daughter used to say, "I'm fighting the tide." She would say this in Florida, partly as a joke, because the local news was always consumed with what was going on in the Gulf. The diurnal tides, for example. The dreaded red tides. But Teddy never fit in with her peers and actively resisted their preferences:

- The music they listened to.
- The clothing they wore.
- Their straight, center-parted hair.

Teddy took some pride in the fact that she wasn't anything like the girls who tormented her.

She was fighting the tide.

Maybe Teddy was still fighting it.

"I know," Flo used to say. Although she didn't, not really.

Teddy has always been slight, and agile of mind, she has always been separate. Perhaps she is a genius. Perhaps she is cruel. Teddy is certainly unlike anyone Flo has ever known, and if Flo doesn't always know what to say to her daughter, still she longs for exactly the right words.

17

The third daughter! Her name was Ksenia, which means Wanderer. It also means Hospitable, which was why Ksenia's mother had chosen it—wouldn't a hospitable soul, after all, be welcomed anywhere?

Ksenia was different: small and quick and subject to terrible dreams. From the earliest age she had to guard against what might come into her head. She was deathly afraid of water, and yet water of any kind—indeed, even the color blue, because water was blue, wasn't it?—exerted a tremendous and confusing pull. Not everyone understood her. Up to this point she had been protected from the world by her sisters and especially her mother, who loved her like the mother bear. This was the child she had gotten, after all.

"You can be in the world but not of it," Ksenia's mother counselled. "You can be patient when you need to." When it came Ksenia's turn to take her leave, the girl was afraid.

"Do not be afraid," Ksenia's mother told her. "You will find what you need."

"I must go into the world, Mother," Ksenia said sadly.

"Don't be afraid," her mother repeated. "I will tell you what to do, and what not to do."

18

WALKING FOR DOG, *to* Dog, Flo passes a large indoor mall. Its exterior walls are concrete, stained now; inside the mall, seniors tramp past the storefronts again and again. They wear soft jogging pants and brightly colored walking shoes that look inflated. Other malls in the area are failing, but this one always has cars in the lot, and so what Flo thinks now is, "Well, Friend, you will live another day." The mall has its own, real name, but to Flo it is, it will always be, Friend. (Flo has many Friends. She *does*!)

Flo pauses, she takes another look at Teddy's note. This part she has already read but there's the mall, right there.

"You used to make me go shopping," Teddy says. "What was that all about?" (What *was* that about? It was about shared experience, Flo thought. But it's true: Teddy hated to shop. Especially for clothing. She was happiest in old flannel shirts, in T-shirts and those long boys' skater shorts made of slippery nylon. Also true: Flo had made her go to the mall, sometimes. This was near the end, after Teddy started high school.)

Perhaps after a while Flo just should have given up. But here was the thing: every year in the summer Flo and her own mother used to go to the giant indoor shopping center near their house. It was a tradition Flo still remembers with something approaching yearning. They'd set out early, they'd stay all day. That mall was something: There was a waterfall you could walk under! There were great cushioned benches in fanciful shapes, candy colored. One time Flo's mother bought Flo a pin with a picture of a terrier on it, and one time they found Flo a black-and-white checked shirt that she felt really good in—it had the tab sleeves that rolled up and buttoned, it was fitted. Flo wore it until it was a rag.

As a teen, Flo honestly liked spending time with her mother. She preferred it to the company of her friends, in fact. While Flo liked her friends, they could be treacherous, and Flo never worried if her mom actually liked spending time with her. There was never anything to prove. They shared a name, but it was more than that. "Why did you name me what you did?" little Flo asked her mother once. "Oh, I had to name you something," her mother said, almost airily. "I had to name you so that your story could begin."

Flo's mother is dead, but Flo still likes the mall, any mall. This one, here, is well lit, and the people still come. The crowds are comforting, being generally cheerful. And this: you can buy a stuffed animal (a plushie) if you want to.

The mall opens its doors even before the stores do so that people can do their walking there. This early-morning event is called Walking Club. Some people bring their dogs—Flo has seen this. She has never tried Walking Club, with or without Dog, although she appreciates its value. Flo understands the solace it might bring.

19

AN OLDER COUPLE is looking for their car in the mall parking lot. Flo knows them from The Mutiny; they come in once a week during the senior hour to buy milk (organic) and frozen dinners (also organic).

They recognize her, too, or at least the man does. "Hello!" he cries to Flo, who is walking briskly along the sidewalk; after a moment's hesitation the woman joins him in a wave, smiling. The sidewalk is poorly maintained here, a strange lost thing between the four-lane road and the mall. Flo, poorly maintained also, waves back. Why not? This couple, they are predictable to a point with their milk and their dinners, but sometimes they buy bread so dense with grain, with fiber, the loaf is an anvil. A kedge. Sometimes they buy fresh fruit.

Flo cannot always anticipate their purchases, the way she can with some of the other patrons. She assumes they know what they need, that they each know what the other needs, and she is, honestly, a little envious of this. She is drawn to this idea of them, also.

20

What to pack, for her daughter? For the child who was the hardest, her Special, and perhaps—her instincts suggested—most in need of protection?

Ksenia's mother, who had not worried about her two older girls, could only hope she had adequately prepared her youngest for the world that waited. In all its brutal beauty.

21

FLO DOESN'T REALLY WANT to engage with the couple outside of work like this; she has Dog to find. And the encounter? It makes her shy. Or maybe cornered. In this way she is like Teddy; in this way she is like a wild animal.

After the incident, the Ephrem locals said Teddy was feral. Not that being feral is necessarily a bad thing. To Flo at least, who sincerely loves the many feral cats in this city that is like a suburb. They seem to live on every block. They take shelter from the day's heat, but every night, Flo can hear them banging around.

Some people fear the ferals, but B. collects them. For instance, she brought Flo the cat with the folded ear. That was Minnow, who is diffident. Flo lies to her landlord that she has exactly three animals. The landlord probably knows different but Flo's apartment does not *smell* like animal. That is the important thing.

She is very careful with the feeding of the cats, Dog, the guinea pig B.'s sister's grandchild forgot to love. She gets a discount at The Mutiny, and buys the high-protein pet food. About her own food, Flo is sometimes less particular, though when Teddy was still home, she tried to take care. She kept the fridge stocked. Sometimes Teddy helped with this.

"Teddy, pick up some milk then," Flo might have said. But maybe sometimes Teddy didn't want to get the milk or there was something that kept her from thinking of it.

"From the grocery, right?" The woman calls to her from the parking lot, still smiling. "I almost didn't recognize you."

"I'm from the grocery, yes! Yes, yes, good to see you."

The woman regards Flo's sweatshirt, her red shoes. "You

look different," she says, adding quickly, "not that that's a bad thing."

Flo used to be comfortably padded but she has become very thin since living here. Her skin is dry and webbed as a cantaloupe. It is as pale as an infant's.

She was named after her mother, and now she is the age her mother was when Flo was a girl—older, even. Flo was the kind of child who played with dolls long after her peers had moved on to lipstick and boys. To their own lives and the prisons they made of them.

Getting older is like being in a strange land.

"Times change," Flo says to the woman, shrugging apologetically. She means to keep things light.

22

Ten years ago Flo might not have imagined herself working at a grocery store, but here she is, and she is well liked at The Mutiny, by staff and by the customers. In fact, she has received excellent performance reviews. She allows herself a small pride in these assessments, in the relevance and competence they recognize. The trust, even, that they represent.

"It's so funny to run into you like this!" the woman exclaims. "What are you doing, walking around here?" Everyone drives in this town, everyone but Flo, is what she is saying.

"Oh well," Flo says in her joking voice. She has left the sidewalk, ventured into a no-man's-land of dead grass between the sidewalk and the parking lot, the better to hear. "I'm the same everywhere, always on my feet."

"You just look different," the woman persists.

"You should have known me back when," Flo says, thinking of the old ways, her life as a social worker. "I lived in the Midwest. I wore clip-on earrings." Flo laughs. "Talk about different!"

The woman cocks her head. Maybe she just can't make out what Flo is saying. A good ten feet still separates them, and Flo resists moving closer, being ready, as she is, for the conversation to end.

"I like my job." Flo raises her voice to be heard. "I used to do something else, is all."

At The Mutiny, Flo stocks shelves, she rings up the pricey coffee, she helps the gentleman with a tremor and a walker get his groceries to the car. It is a wonder to her that she was once a social worker at all, though at the time she had been confident in that work, also. She thought she was good at it, people said she had a knack, but then the business with Teddy happened and Flo couldn't explain how she'd missed what was right before her. How damaged her daughter really was.

"We all have our blind spots." Sunby used to say this; he said it long before Teddy did.

The couple from The Mutiny are well dressed for their morning at the mall, the man in a collared shirt, the woman in a pretty light cardigan. They are typical of the clientele Flo works with. A little fussy. Used to seeing the world in a certain way. Used to getting what they want. They usually look so happy. They look happy now!

Flo finds this remarkable; they've clearly lived long enough for things to have happened to them. To those they love. Flo wonders if, when Teddy comes, her girl will be happy. Not like these people, exactly, but happy in a Teddy way would be enough. Then she tells herself not to want for things she can't necessarily have.

23

Ksenia's mother gave her:

- *A flask of vinegar.*
- *A bottle of beer.*
- *A loaf of her good bread, heavy with seeds and sliced thickly.*

"There is no butter for your bread," Ksenia's mother said. "Not yet. But see what you find." Then she kissed her daughter and turned away before Ksenia could see her weeping. The leaving had to happen, Ksenia's mother knew. It was the way of things, her own wishes hardly mattering. She kept her tears in. But later, when she was alone, her face became puffy with crying, and it stayed this way for three hours. No, for three long days.

Gods! Ksenia was her pet and a bit strange in the world. Not everyone understood her.

Just as not everyone understood Ksenia's mother, who though accustomed to this wanted something different for her favorite child.

24

"WHAT?" THE WOMAN has cupped a hand to her ear and so Flo moves closer. Her foot hits a spangled rock and her ankle turns sharply, enough to hurt. The pain is a spark. "Damn it!"

Flo wants to be slow and calm. When it comes, her rage is unpleasant. Berserker it is, coming from a place she refuses to acknowledge. For a long time Flo believed, she *hoped*, that she could leave that part of herself behind. She kept moving, from place to place. But she was like a character in one of her mother's stories, and so of course all the parts of her always followed after.

When Teddy was little, she had a temper, too. An electricity came off her at those times, she became silent and cold; it was not a child's heat. And so it was not something to joke about. Even then, Charlie and Flo had known this. There was also that wildness: Teddy's wide light eyes that looked naked, framed as they were with those white white lashes. Neither of them understood their daughter, exactly. Of course Flo worried, but this was the child they had made.

"Are you okay?" This from the woman, but Flo catches her balance, she waves.

"I'm fine!"

It's too late to just turn around and keep walking, this conversation seeming determined not to end. Flo hobbles through trash toward the couple where they wait at the edge of the mall parking lot. It's a decent mall in a good neighborhood, but even here, apparently, it is hard to keep up. She passes a block of cement from which rebar extends, willy-nilly. Here is one sock. There is a branch.

This last is from the line of southern live oaks someone has planted along the edge of the parking lot, for shade. Flo strides with what she means to be sociable confidence, because she's trying to act the way she wants to feel (except for the limp). For example, she wants to be thought of as a friendly person. She does not want to think that Dog might be gone.

"I'm fine!" Flo cries out again.

She remembers how Dog came to her. The way one day it wasn't there, the next it was, hanging and minge-ing around the garage, whining when Flo went to check on her car, which starts when it wants to, which is rarely. This was—how long ago? Maybe two years, now.

The dog had a stealth about it. Also a gentleness, a sadness. Its red-caramel fur was stiff, as if with sweat, and almost resignedly Flo began to leave food for it. The dog seemed to have all its teeth, though it was no longer young.

"Be careful there!" This from the man, the man in the collared shirt.

One early morning, Flo was standing outside with her tea. There was nowhere to sit, so she stood, and she saw that the dog had come into the side yard. The gate wasn't broken yet; later she would find the hole dug under the chain-link. The dog stood perfectly still, one front paw lifted; watching it, Flo crouched and set down her mug slowly onto the patio, and in that light the mug despite its rainbow looked like concrete also. The dog edged closer and together Flo and the dog looked at the mug. Flo stayed softly still; she felt quiet and happy in that moment. Then she stood and showed the dog the spines of the pencil cholla. "Be careful of this," she warned. The dog listened with interest, then sniffed at the cactus; Flo could see that it understood. Later she told Sunby, she told B., that she was pretty sure the dog winked at her. Later she would think Dog's appearance particularly fortuitous. And mysterious. Occult, even.

"Well, come along, Dog," Flo had said. When the dog came inside the house, the cats tolerated him. His rusty smell. The plumes of fur on his hindquarters, like trousers. She lets him sleep in her room, though not on her bed. She took him in to be fixed. Flo knows cats best; she had not until that moment considered herself a dog person necessarily.

But there was something there. And SilverGirl adored Dog, there was that. Maybe Flo was a dog person after all, she has thought since. Maybe she wasn't a child person, though. Flo has thought this too.

She did not know this dog as a puppy. She has told Dog this. It is important, Flo thinks, to level any expectations.

Flo stops, she steals a glance at the card that is still in her hand. "I expected more from you," Teddy writes. "But that was me, at 14." Was this an acknowledgment of sorts? The pain in Flo's ankle is tiny but bright.

25

"HERE," THE MAN from the couple says. He has picked his way through the garbage littering the brown verge to meet her. "Are you okay? You're limping." He picks up the branch and holds it out to her. "Lean on this."

26

Ksenia began to walk. She had a staff made of hazel in her hand. (A hazel staff? That made sense.) The path she took was an old sea bed, lined with shells, and when Ksenia saw an especially pretty one she would pocket it. She was not unhappy but she was not happy either; when she came upon an old fellow, bald as the moon and sitting by a stile, taking in the sun, she was glad enough.

"Hello, daughter!" he greeted her, and Ksenia called back to him, smiling. She was a kind soul, if awkward, and when she drew nearer she saw how very old the man was, the leather of his face.

She held out her hand to him, and the man took it into the two of his. "Do not ask me my name," he said. "It is not written." And Ksenia in turn did not tell him her name, but she laid down her staff and drew from her pouch the beer that her mother had given her. They shared it, the whole of it, in the sun, without his even asking. The man told her that the beer was precious. Everything in the villages had been drunk, he said: all the vodka, the moonshine. Even the nail polish, society's usual rules having been cast aside.

We learn to adapt, is all. And the beer was good all the time it lasted. But perhaps it was the company, also. Ksenia was drawn to this wizard.

We have to find our people, after all.

27

"How is your daughter?" the mall couple ask. They have established that Flo's ankle is fine (well, Flo says it is). They have decided the weather is warm, but pleasant. Now the three of them stand outside the couple's SUV, which was there near the edge of the parking lot the whole while. The woman holds a soda in a plastic cup hazy with condensation.

"Well," Flo says. "Yes." The branch is certainly nice enough, but of course these people think that Flo and Teddy are like everyone else. They probably think Flo deserves the branch, that she deserves to be comfortable.

"What's your daughter's name again?" the woman asks. She means to be kind, Flo knows this.

"Teddy." Flo shifts her weight; her ankle burns.

"What a beautiful name! So unusual, isn't it?" The woman turns to her husband, then back to Flo. "And how old is she? I should know this!" She titters.

"Old enough to know better," Flo says distractedly. She is trying to remember if the couple have children of their own, or grandchildren even.

"It goes by fast," the woman says, and Flo must remind herself: the woman is just being social. Flo makes herself do the same, though she is bored and suddenly lonely, anxious to resume her search for Dog; she still remembers the rules of polite society that her mother taught her. She dutifully inquires if there are children, and if so how many, what age.

The man looks off into the middle distance as the woman becomes especially animated. "Oh, we have three! Boys. It seems like just yesterday they were born. I remember every detail."

Flo has to think about that a moment. Personally she finds it hard to remember the details of Teddy's birth, it seems so long ago, except that it had been a prolonged labor. But in the end there Teddy was, greasy with vernix. She hadn't been a cute baby, or a winsome toddler; her body was all angles, her hair that hard white blond and in a constant snarl, like a crazy hat. But Teddy's look was unusual, and thus interesting. Flo, who suspected, correctly, that her daughter would age well (Teddy has, and will), wouldn't have known what to do with a proper girl.

"Every age is a joy, isn't it?" the woman says.

"Yes," Flo says uncertainly. There were certainly good times. There were! In fact, sometimes at night, she walks herself through the different stages of her only child's life to remind herself. It is like the reading of a rosary.

- *Baby Teddy:* no one says she is adorable, a darling. But at this age she has an eager look, the look of someone with something going on inside. And. She is so easy! Flo is all amazement, the way her child doesn't cry or carry on the way other babies do. Perhaps Flo is a little smug. See! See what I have made!
- *Small Teddy:* so alone, her eagerness displaced by ruthless solemnity. Her pale eyes are glassy, sensitive to light, and her skin has a translucence to it, which in certain lights seems unwholesome, but in others as if she were lit from within. Her intelligence is undeniably . . . radiant. Radiant. Flo is her best friend (her only). "You are the most beautiful, Mama," Teddy used to say, and Flo knew the flattery came from love. Flo felt loved. Teddy had the capacity for anger, but that great decency too. Flo sees this. Perhaps others don't, to Flo's great sorrow.

- *Teen Teddy:* this is a short chapter they share. As it turns out. Flo cannot hope to know her daughter, though she tries. They eat sweets together. They watch television. Flo knows that people talk. She knows Teddy is viewed as strange. She knows *she* is viewed as strange. But life is strange. This will pass, Flo thinks.

It doesn't pass. But the verdict was involuntary manslaughter, thank gods. And Teddy was a juvenile. It could have been so much worse.

And oh when Teddy was small! She was alert and interested in everything: the cats they had then, thickset Ender and the beautiful tabby Mars. Teddy regarded her sock feet—yellow knit slippers, made by Flo's mother—with attention, because within the yellow wool, somewhere, were the feet she knew. And her hands! Small and sensitive, they would reach for the dangly earrings Flo wore then. One pair in particular, Teddy loved; these were shell-shaped, and made of blue-veined glass that flashed in the light like code when Flo moved her head. Flo cannot remember what became of them. They must have been lost in one of the moves.

She misses those earrings. Among other things.

"I loved when they were small," the woman is saying wistfully. "But the high school years were certainly fun! We got a pool table," she confides. "We wanted our home to be the place our boys came with their friends. And they *did*!"

By the time Teddy entered high school, she had become increasingly wiry and distant. But the violence, Flo never saw it coming. For a while after the incident, Flo didn't always tell people that she had a daughter. Then she did. The stories changed. Some of them were true, or part-true. There was the one about how keen her daughter was, a quick study.

True enough. She didn't go to a regular school, Flo said, and that was true also; Teddy finished her high school education at Juvie. Flo said that public school wasn't big enough to hold Teddy, and that, in its way, was also true.

"I just got this letter," Flo says, apropos of nothing. She waves the card and slides it back into her pocket. Flo has told this couple (what are their *names*?) that Teddy travels for work. Certainly since leaving the facility, Teddy has moved constantly—Flo doesn't always know where. "Wherever you are, I am too," Flo used to tell her daughter, when Teddy was stuck in Juvie and they couldn't live together anymore.

"She's living in Colorado now." Colorado is not mentioned in the card, at least the part Flo has already read. She is, at this point, making shit up.

No, she is trying to tell a story that is not strange, that is pleasing to the couple, to herself. Because she worries that she doesn't know where Teddy is much of the time, she invents places. Some of them are exotic—Flo borrows from her own mother's stories—and there is usually a mountain. In Flo's mind the mountain is blue. And there is the story, how Teddy, barely a teen, had killed a teacher. Perhaps in the context of the other stories Flo tells about her daughter, this one, the true one, might lose some of its fury.

Teddy is well, she says now. As in physical health, and Flo hopes this is true. "She is coming for a visit. Soon. She's been lonely." Flo voice is confident now, Teddy's loneliness being beyond dispute.

"A visit! Lovely!" The woman says this and the man nods. He is already bored. Perhaps, for the couple, life is like a Hallmark movie. Perhaps they imagine Flo and Teddy baking together. Perhaps they are imagining the grandchildren Flo will surely have.

They are not particularly curious, the couple, in any case. Or imaginative. They are not like Teddy, or B., whose sister sent her a MacBook one Christmas in lieu of coming over. Now, whenever B. and Flo have a question about something, B. can look it up. B. is spectacularly good at finding things online. Flo no longer has a cellphone, and she doesn't own a laptop, although she uses the computer at the library and she can borrow B.'s MacBook whenever she wants.

At one time Teddy had a laptop. She needed it for school, and Flo was proud she could get it for her. Every day, Teddy would look up a new word, seemingly at random. Flo was charmed by this! One day Flo walked past Teddy's open laptop. Flo doesn't remember where Teddy was. It was just Flo and the laptop. The laptop beamed, lambent and quick-witted, and on the screen was the definition of the word "anthropomorphism." This was before any of the business with Mrs. Benedict, and Flo was hopeful for Teddy's prospects. She was hopeful for her own. Then, Teddy had returned from wherever she'd been and slammed the laptop shut.

But Flo understood. Teddy was a teenager and a girl needed her privacy.

28

They drank the beer, sharing it back and forth, and after a time the wizard, smiling, asked the same question he had asked twice before: "Am I handsome, daughter?"

Ksenia had just taken a mouthful of beer, yeasty and cool, and she wiped her mouth. She set the bottle down, the better to study the wizard's face. The old man was as he had been before: skin of his neck hanging loose, back still bent. His feet were huge as bear paws. ***Polar bear*** *paws, Flo's mother had always insisted.*

"You are as you should be," Ksenia said. "You can be no other way."

And this is where Ksenia's journey really began.

The wizard nodded, and his face did not change a jot when he told her to walk southwest, for three nights and three days. "The sun is young at day's beginning. Look for him, and he will guide you cheerfully and well throughout the day," he said. "On the third day you will find something."

Ksenia thanked him sincerely, and the old man bowed to her, his bald pate as speckled as the bullfinch's egg. From his robes he produced a brick of butter; while she watched he drew waxed cotton from another pocket. He used this to wrap the butter, and he tied the whole thing in twine.

"For your bread or better," he said. "You go your way and I will go mine." And so Ksenia accepted the gift. She picked up her hazel staff and carried on.

29

"How are your pets?" the couple ask now. They have two lovebirds at home; sometimes they buy berries at The Mutiny for the birds to eat. They know Flo lives with animals also.

"Oh they are exactly themselves," Flo says. "You know?" She scratches at her neck and the woman's eyes are drawn to the eczema, then dart away.

"Not really," she says primly, adjusting her cardigan, and Flo is reminded why animals are preferable to some people; she is never lonely in the company of animals, for one thing. And animals make Flo feel as she did with her mother, with Sunby, with Teddy before she grew up. Which is to say, accepted unconditionally.

She opens her mouth to explain but the woman, whatever her name is, says, "Our lovebirds, now? They are cute as ever." The woman is extremely graceful, her sweater an impeccable mint green; her face, lined, looks wise beneath a neat silver cap of hair. Still, this is what she comes up with: "Just as cute as pie," she says.

Dog, Flo thinks. "Yeah, well," she says. "Lovebirds."

She doesn't mean to sound snotty.

"My dog is missing," she adds impulsively.

"Oh, dear!" the woman cries.

"And my friend just died," Flo adds.

"I'm sorry!" Now the man is paying attention again.

"And I'm not really sure my daughter visiting is a good idea."

A darkling notion.

"At least the mall is still open," Flo adds when the couple remain silent. "At least it's not one of those dead malls." It can still be a good day, is what she is saying.

The woman is staring pointedly now, at Flo, at the raw place on her neck where the eczema begins. The sweatshirt can't hide it; there might even be a little blood. She touches her own neck and exchanges a meaningful glance with her husband.

"I have to go," Flo says abruptly.

"Well now," the woman says. "We'd better be getting along, too." Her voice less friendly now; she and her husband climb into their Land Rover and pull away before the man, who's driving, is even buckled in. Flo guesses they live nearby: the mall is ringed by apartments for people aged 55+. The apartments are expensive. Flo isn't even 55 yet—she's 54! and strapped for cash!—but she sometimes imagines what that would be like, living here in the better, light-filled apartments near the mall. If she could afford the apartment, she would have money to burn at the mall.

And what would she buy there—candy?

Candy. Maybe a chocolate Jesus, because Jesus as an adult was cool, even if Sunby could never convince her of the God's Son business. Sunby! Flo wants everything to be different. She wants her friend to be alive, she wants Dog to amble across the parking lot, she wants to want Teddy to visit. And *was* there such a thing as a chocolate Jesus? Surely there was.

And maybe, if so much good luck could happen, Flo would find a skirt at the mall, the kind she's always wanted, made of tulle crackling with sparkles. And Nell and Sunby would come visit her here. Sunby: Flo could tell him anything. She couldn't shock him if she tried, and he wouldn't drive away, not in a Land Rover, not in anything else. He and Nell would come to her, they would appear at her door, and the door would be blue; the visit would be a surprise but also absolutely natural. They would play board games, the three of them, or four, if B. came over too, in one of the crisp white mall-side apartments Flo has seen through shining window glass.

Dog would lie at her feet, hoping for snacks. SilverGirl would lie on her lap, eating the snacks.

And—Flo puts her hand to her neck—there was room for Teddy in this dream. Flo would be living in the bright, beautiful space, gyring in her tulle. She'd throw the blue door wide for her daughter and there would be no doubt. Never doubt. "You came just in time for the next game!" she might cry.

There is a game Sunby always liked, played with cards and cardboard gems. Sunby always won, though Flo suspects Nell let him win, again and again, such was his delight when he did.

They'd play that game. Here. Near the mall.

Sunby and Nell; what they shared was like a light. Nell was at least a decade younger than Sunby but that didn't seem to make a difference. They went out for chicken every Sunday, the two of them, and before Flo left Ephrem she went with them. She became part of their magic circle. The place was Hetty's TakeOut and the chicken was tender.

"This is why I could never be a vegetarian," Sunby said. His chin shone with grease.

For a while in Ephrem, Flo had kept chickens. She loved them until she butchered and ate them. After not too long, that became confusing and so she bought rotisserie chickens at the market.

Flo does not have a skirt that sparkles. She will never eat a chocolate Jesus. And the couple? Their Land Rover is likely *filled* with chocolate deities! They probably bite off the heads and throw the rest away.

I'm a freak, Flo thinks. *They think I am a freak.*

But Dog waits for her to find him, at The Place, surely he does. And the branch is a walking stick; she sees the way it fits her hand. There's that.

Flo watches the couple drive away. They are just people, she reminds herself. They are only human.

30

Flo's father was only human. Once he hit her in the face, but his hand was open because he loved her. He told little Flo, "I just want you to know what it feels like to be alive." Flo, in her Garanimals tank top and shorts set, would go fetch her poppa at the bar.

She had three shorts sets, and the tops were striped. She always wore the proper-colored shirt with the right shorts. (What would happen if she didn't? Little Flo didn't want to find out.) And fetching her poppa? It was just something Flo had to do. But not something Teddy had to do, not ever, Flo made sure of that.

Sometimes Flo's dad bought her a ginger ale with a cherry in it. Sometimes, walking home, he'd teach her songs—"Stardust," "Paper Doll," "Sentimental Journey"—all these songs from another time. He'd sing them with her if he wasn't too drunk or sad or mean. Poppa hated women, but he was proud of his daughter; even at six, Flo knew this. So she sang. He was out of their lives before she turned seven. Flo's mother left, and she took Flo with her.

Poppa's liver went, and then his heart. But that was later.

Flo had sworn she'd do it all differently. When Teddy was little, radiant as a lantern, they would sit side by side on the couch and read together or watch the TV. A light passed between them when they did that, something primeval and good that Flo trusted. They shared that. Nothing can change that they had that, once.

It wasn't that Flo was perfect. Though the anger, it might be useful also.

And Flo's moods could dive; there were times she would go into her room, climb into bed, and stay there. She called it *stayabed*. Flo always told Teddy that she would be back and she always kept this promise, emerging smiling—after an hour, or a day. Flo liked to think that she told her daughter the truth of things.

And mostly she did, except for the times when she, Flo, was just trying to survive. There was no room for truth, then, or even accuracy.

31

FLO RETURNS to her sidewalk. She is limping but she distracts herself by naming, in her head, things she does not miss:

- Poppa.
- The girls Teddy knew in school.
- The winter. Especially the winter.

She has the staff and she needs it, whether she deserves it or not. She has a sweatshirt. Flo stops for a moment and hugs herself.

32

THE DESERT can get cold at night, but it doesn't snow here. When they lived in Ephrem, the snow was apocalyptic, piling past the sill of the bay window on the first level of the house so that the living room became dim as a cave for weeks. Teddy turned on all the lights then and she helped Flo clean the walks. Their breath froze and snaked skyward like smoke; the winter light guttered like a candle. Flo remembers the way that light played across the plowed fields, which filled with snow early, furrows first outlined then hidden till spring.

Before Ephrem there had been Florida and the diurnal tides of the Gulf. Flo and Teddy lived in Tallahassee, at least this side of the blue door they did. It was here Flo got her social work degree, at night, on weekends, whenever she could manage it. The Gulf was a short drive away from where they lived and there was no winter to speak of, although the palm trees could seem unwholesome, their fronds brown at the edges and rattling like a bird's bones. Maybe Flo doesn't much miss Florida, either. But it was in Ephrem where the hard knot of her little family had unraveled so quickly.

Flo is not cynical. It is not in her nature. It is not in the nature of the stories she grew up on. Those myths. Despite everything, Flo persists in her beliefs. What are they?

- She tried her best with Teddy.
- Sunby was a good human. And B.! She is good. Flo's mother also. (These are three good people, then.)
- Animals are a mystery but not in the way humans are. Animals, so far as Flo can tell, never judge.

Dog, Flo thinks. She resumes walking.

33

She walked and she walked, sleeping hard in the night and rising with the sun, who was cheerful in the morning as the old wizard had promised, and raced across the sky with all the energy of youth. Every morning Ksenia gripped her hazel staff anew, pointing her feet in the direction the old wizard had suggested. Sometimes she thought about her sisters, or her mother. Sometimes she thought about nothing at all.

On the third day she came upon a great mountain. Its rock face was tall and brooding but a path was cut into the side. She followed this path to its end, where she found a house that seemed to grow right out of the rock on which it stood. No animals grazed outside—there was no grass—but kites and eagles wheeled about the rock house. When they saw Ksenia they flew to greet her, although she couldn't understand their language any more than Severina could.

34

No one else knew Derrykin, which is how Teddy and Flo liked it. They'd talk and it was their secret; it set them apart, united. In fact Flo used to brag, just a little, back when she still felt she could, that from a young age Teddy grasped English but also other languages intuitively. That's why she can create a language, Flo used to say. Her brain is flexible that way.

And as a baby, Teddy had been pliant, period. Flo would take her on long walks, Teddy in her stroller, and the sun would cast its dappled light; it was almost like being alone. The only other people Flo can—*could*—be with in this way? Her mom. And Sunby, of course. (Someday it will be like this with B., although Flo doesn't know it yet.)

An easy baby, people said, and Flo had been able to comfort her daughter then. Teddy became a toddler, and the world had not marked her yet.

Later, Teddy would grind her teeth; she had to have mouthguards. It was stress, the dentist said. Teddy clenched her teeth during the day and they rocked in their sockets. The bacteria got in. Her gums bled. More stress, the dentist said. Yes, Flo said, hating the girls who caused her daughter misery.

Those girls. Awful, like flatfish. And Flo's response to them was a chill, her hair follicles tightening and rising. Each day Teddy came home she was lonelier than the day before; she was (Flo later realized) the loneliest person in the world. And Flo? She felt bigger at these times, a giant in a fairy tale.

But though she could have lifted a car off an infant, or kicked a stout door in, there were no cars to lift, no doors to break. No blue doors, even, to escape through. She'd be waiting for Teddy to get home, tugging the curtains aside to peek out, and she was sick at her stomach, thinking about what her daughter's day might have been. Anticipating that first glimpse of Teddy's face and what it might reveal. Anticipating what she, Flo, might have to conceal.

Because the pretty headscarf Flo wore? Red and yellow, it practically rose up from her head in these times. She was that scared. She was that angry. It was something ancient that puffed her up, she figured, left over from when we were furry. But she didn't know what to do with it. This was Florida.

"Be in this world but not of it," she said to Teddy then. At the time, she thought she succeeded in keeping the hopelessness out of her voice. Looking back now, she is less certain.

Sometimes Flo wishes that Teddy would write to her about *that*. Sometimes Flo wants proof that anything she said made a difference.

Flo is alert to everything around her as she walks away from the mall. Her red shoes make their nicking slipping sound, but she listens carefully beyond that for the sounds the dog will make when he is hungry, or lonely: a grunting. Would Dog be by the mall? This seems fantastical, but perhaps some cook, or a shopkeeper, would feed him. That's something Flo, or B., or Sunby would do, after all, or the well-meaning grocer in another of the stories Flo's mother used to tell. Flo keeps walking, keeps listening. He could be anywhere. Those sounds—his sounds—will lead her to him.

A day or so ago, this was after Sunby died, Flo had a dream about sound. In the dream, she was in the desert. It was night, and cool—almost cold. But the moon kindly shone its reflected light, and Flo could hear the night sounds, which in this dream were a sort of music. All the different animal and plant voices chiming together.

In the dream, Flo somehow knew this was the voice of the earth, and when she woke she felt a sympathy and a calm that clung to her for hours after. The dream seemed to be about harmony, and Flo felt that Sunby in some way was responsible for it. This thought was a consolation. And the dream made her feel closer to the desert, to her life in this place.

Because Flo isn't always sure she likes it here. Of course it is hard to think of moving again: Each move requires its own courage. Each move takes its toll. In Ephrem, the fecundity of the land was almost alarming. In November, they were shooting the deer.

Here the sun beats, a strong heart. It has its uses; it can be fierce.

The dream reminds her of the respite night can bring to a desert place.

Flo usually tells B. about her dreams, but this she keeps for herself.

35

Night came quickly and early in this place, but the sun, which grew to an old man by each day's end, was still holding court when the door to the rock house opened slowly. A clear blue, this door was. Out came a creature, as broad as an elephant and tall as two men together. He was something, his jaw long and hinged, and on his head two horns curled in on themselves. His hide was rough and the color of earth. He had two great brown eyes with a bit of blood in them, but also a third eye, blue as the door, and luminous. This eye was centered in his forehead and shone like the sun. The creature's hooves looked dangerous and beautiful both—sharp, they glittered as if brushed in diamond.

Ksenia was wonderfully afraid. ("Was it a chimera?" Flo used to ask, because she loved Greek myths, even at that age, and her mother would say, this was no chimera.) Ksenia had to look away from the blue eye because of its color.

It was quiet on the mountain, but when the creature spoke it was like bells ringing. "Let us go," he said. "Let us see together what the future brings."

36

"Tomorrow is another day," Flo used to say to Teddy. Flo tries to picture her daughter arriving at the apartment—not tomorrow but soon enough—greeting the animals, greeting her mother with joy. Flo closes her eyes and imagines Teddy's skinny arms closing around her.

Her ankle hurts. Her throat is dry. Her shoulders and the side of her neck are raw, and as she walks she touches the sore scaly flesh, again and again. She can't help it.

The sweatshirt rubbing so that finally she pulls it off and ties it around her waist.

"Be strong and endure," Flo's mother would tell her. "One day this pain will be of use." It was something she'd seen on a poster and it made a strong impression. The words also impressed young Flo, who years later would repeat them to her own daughter, during the years in Florida, and even in Ephrem for a while.

Flo herself has learned that you get through one day. Then you get through another. Time is a trickster, but you do your best. For example, sometimes Flo will be in the middle of some stupid task, something she hates—like laundry, or the vacuuming, say—and she'll imagine herself on a beach, walking, the smell of the water, when . . . it is suddenly dinnertime, task complete and the day almost done. The relief in that. "I got through it," Flo has thought proudly, even when things were at their worst.

But sometimes it's the other way, as it was during Teddy's court trial, when the Ephrem locals, who loved Mrs. Benedict or at the very least claimed to, were so angry and congregated outside Flo's trilevel, her and Teddy's house, and they were on *bullhorns*. Yelling who knows what; Flo can't remember it, or she won't.

She would get up the next day and the crowd would be gone, but one time someone had spray-painted the word *Freak* on the garage door. And Flo, who learned then, if she hadn't already, how hard it is not to get sealed into someone else's version of who you are, went back inside and set herself to working and working. Because at least that was something to do, something to keep the mind occupied even if the work was *cleaning a drawer,* for godsake. She was controlling the narrative. She was trying to. And Flo will never forget this: she looked at the clock and it was five minutes past the last time she'd checked. Nowhere near lunchtime, and here she was already looking forward to night because that would be the end of another day.

And there was this. After Teddy went to Juvie, when Flo was still in Ephrem, she grimly cleared away photos of her daughter from the house; the pictures made her too sad. Removing the photos seemed proof of something—her own distance, perhaps. (Are we ever not responsible for what our children do? But *I* didn't kill Mrs. Benedict, Flo insisted to Sunby once. Or twice. Perhaps three times, but nothing she said changed anything, for Teddy or for herself. Or for Mrs. Benedict, who was, of course, still dead.)

Flo didn't throw the photos away—not the one of Teddy on a bike, knees rusted with scabs (she was a fearless, reckless child), or the second-grade class picture, plastic barrettes just barely holding back Teddy's bangs (she had been growing them out, it took forever). Flo took these framed pictures with her every time she moved. They are in a laundry bag in her closet, safe, but she can't see them so they can't hurt her heart.

This was not the same as not caring. Because it still pained her to think of them, shut away like that.

37

The creature's hide was furred but also scaled, the scales green like oily water, and erupting from the clumps of fur this way and that. Ksenia touched one, gently, and the creature shied away before saying calmly, That is enough. Climb up. Ksenia slung her staff over her back; taking great fistfuls of fur, she tried to lift herself up, but she made no progress, even when he knelt to meet her. Then she remembered the thick bread her mother had given her. She pressed the slices into the creature's fur and they became like steps, which she climbed quickly.

At once the creature began to run. He galloped behind the rock house and there was a path that went up up up; Ksenia grabbed onto his horns and pressed herself forward, taking care to avoid the scales on the creature's back and shoulders. Ksenia could see now that they were hard as mineral crusts, and inflamed. She was afraid but as the creature galloped and chuffed, gaining momentum, she marveled at the land they traveled through. The creature leaped a river that was gray and pink, thick with salmon (Ksenia closed her eyes against the water). He skirted a gorge, and above them another mountain rose with its blanket of aspen and maple. On the creature ran.

Ksenia had questions. What are you? Where do we travel? Are you fierce or afraid? (Little Flo used to have questions, too, although her mother would simply pause and stare, then continue with the story. And Flo, she ***still*** *has questions, doesn't she?) But the creature ran so hard across the precipices, his hooves ringing on stone, that Ksenia's words were only half heard. And when he ran, muted, on moss, the wind carried Ksenia's words away. Even if he heard, perhaps the creature didn't understand what she* *was asking. She leaned close and gripped the horns more securely. Dusk was falling in earnest now. Ksenia could no longer see the world clearly, or her place in it.*

38

Flo looks up. The sky is bigger here, it seems bigger than it did in the Midwest. It is often a startling blue, as it is today, the clouds well formed, and under that expanse Flo sometimes (often) feels small. She had arrived in Ephrem larger than life, but what happened there diminished her. It made her into a different person who might or might not grow back into the shape she had been.

But she's still here. For a while, after the incident, Flo had wanted to die. She didn't, of course. Here she is.

Why are we afraid of dying? Sunby used to say. Nothing is born, nothing dies. There is only transformation. A cloud becomes rain, he said. Neither is better in itself. "When I die I will cease being this"—here Sunby described himself in the air with a hand—"and I will become something else." Sunby said this transformation was joyful, or could be. It did not have to bring sorrow. He said these things dispassionately, as though his interest were purely professional, and perhaps it was.

Sunby was just a human, but he was wise, Flo thought. He'd never had children, but he understood Teddy. How could that be? "Well, I was someone's child," Sunby said. "And we are all God's children." He shrugged; he knew Flo didn't believe in God. But he did. And Flo, well, she believed in Sunby.

There is no one way to be, Flo understood. She didn't like it, but she understood it.

39

PAST THE MALL, there is a park with three climbing gyms. Perhaps Dog is there, resting in the shade of a climbing ramp. Or. He likes children; perhaps he is playing there, right now, with a child who is kind. Flo turns off the sidewalk and climbs a dry hill, favoring her ankle. She reaches the summit and surveys the park, with its ladders and slides, everything painted in rainbow colors.

Teddy would have hated it here as a child. She didn't like places where other children congregated.

In this way she was like her father, who did not enjoy children, any children, until he had one of his own. And then he only liked Teddy. If she'd had any friends, he wouldn't have liked them. He told Flo so.

Charlie. Sometimes Flo imagines her ex's lean frame gone soft. His hair thinner, or whiter. When they met, in a bar, both in their unassailable 20s, Charlie's hair had been satin black with the blue lights in it; he was vain about that hair, spending time brushing it as a woman might. Perhaps he thought it would save him.

He was almost handsome, and charming when he chose to be. When Teddy lived with Flo, those months after getting out of Juvie, it was clear she longed to hear from her father. It was clear she wished she knew him.

Flo never speaks against Charlie, though she doesn't defend him to her daughter, either. Once Teddy said, "I am like Dad." This was years ago; Teddy might have been in elementary school. "I don't see it," Flo had said bluntly. "You are like me, sweetie." She said this because at that time she wanted it to be so.

Well.

After the incident with Mrs. Benedict, when the people of Ephrem judged her as much as they judged Teddy, Flo wanted to say, "Teddy is only half me!" Even now, she reminds herself that she never said these words out loud, not even to Sunby.

Under the climbing gyms in the park is a sort of padded ground cover made of rubber. Wet pour rubber, it's called, to cushion children if they fall. It's a nice sentiment, Flo thinks.

But some things cannot be safeguarded against. Some things cannot be prevented. For example, there had been a second child, or the promise of one. Flo miscarried after three months and Charlie's response was to grow sick in spirit, as if something fundamental within him had broken. He got stuck in the thorns, Charlie did, his drinking stepping up to the point where he was routinely, suspiciously, shiny-eyed; that was when Flo became impatient. Never sentimental, she was ready to get on with things. They had the one child, and Teddy was enough: bright and hard, like a coin. Like Flo.

Teddy was three when Flo packed their things. They left Charlie sleeping off a bender with the covers rucked up, one sinewy white leg extending out from under a quilt as green as glass. Flo had always hated that quilt, and she was glad to take leave of it. She had stopped loving Charlie some time before. This was in Bakersfield, at least Flo thinks it was, around the time in Flo's life when the losses started totting up, and there wasn't always something to replace what had gone missing. The people. The earrings. The magic. But it was only in looking back later that Flo understood this to be the case.

Not too long after she'd left Charlie—as soon as they got to Tallahassee, actually—Flo found it hard to remember his face. She could not remember the smell of him. At the time, this didn't bother her.

Teddy had her own lanolin smell, underlaid by a sharpness, like arugula. It was deeply part of her. For a while after Teddy was sent away to Juvie, Flo slept in her daughter's bed to feel close to her. She slept there until the sheets no longer smelled of Teddy. They smelled like Flo. She washed them then, and they were never quite the same.

40

All parks are different, Flo thinks. Also they are the same. Dog is not here in any case, this park being empty except for a mother and her little boy. The woman is sitting on a bench, drinking coffee, one of those young happy mothers. She looks nice, whatever that means, and the boy, probably about four, rolls around on the rubber matting like a young bear. The child is jolly, his mother disheveled, which makes Flo like her, it makes her think that maybe this one she won't scare off. Not like the mothers in Florida, who were polite enough but seemed nonplussed, even disapproving.

She hovers next to the bench. She wants to ask this woman if she's seen Dog.

Oh, those women in Florida! They were perfection, weren't they, their stingy lips plumped? The ubiquitous, tiresome conceit of yoga pants. Such dainty tyrants! But this woman has an uneven part and her hair is a tad greasy; she wears jeans that pull tight across her thighs. They probably fit better before the kid was born; they may never fit well again, Flo thinks. When the woman glances up, her smile is genuine. "Hey," she says. Flo nods and edges closer.

"Would you like to join us?" the woman asks. "I feel like I know you from somewhere. The Bounty, maybe?"

"Yep," Flo says. She doesn't remember this young woman, but that's okay. It's nice to be recognized. "That's me."

"You're limping," the woman says. "You want to sit for a bit?" The woman scoots over on the bench, and extracts a plastic baggie filled with goldfish crackers from a canvas backpack. "Snack?"

"Why not?" Flo sits down and it's a relief to get the weight off her ankle. "I've been looking for—"

"Raaaaa!" the little boy roars. He leaps up and hops over to the bench on one foot. "I'm Judah!" he bellows.

"Hello, Judah," Flo says mildly. Judah's mother shakes the bag of crackers. "Here you go, T-Rex," she says to her son. Judah takes a fistful of crackers and hops away.

"I'm Taylor," the woman says. She sets the crackers between them and extends her hand.

"Teddy."

The lie just flies out of her mouth, Flo doesn't even know why. She reaches out to shake hands; she takes a few crackers (which are sticky), to be polite.

"My husband is in New York for work," Taylor says. "I'm trying to keep us busy." She nods at her son, and Flo notices the purple crescents under her eyes, but then Taylor smiles. "It's just us two. Kinda sweet in some ways, you know?"

"I do," Flo says.

For many years it had been just the two of them, Teddy and Flo. The way Flo saw it, Charlie wasn't there to drag them down, and she has some good memories from that time: she and Teddy watching television, eating pizza heaped with olives. The olives had pimentos in them, what Teddy called taillights. Flo would slice up onions to add to the pizza too, making Teddy laugh by first biting into the onion, eating it for its own sake like an apple or a pear.

They also ate cheese fizz, which is what they called cheese you squirt from a can. And donut sundaes, where you put a scoop of plain vanilla ice cream on a donut, any donut, then tart the whole thing up with peanuts, or M&Ms, or chocolate sauce. "Donut bar!" Teddy would shout, and Flo wondered if she could be forgiven, thinking her daughter was happy then.

Sometimes, if there was no chocolate sauce, they would eat their donuts with butter; there was always butter. They were like a couple of college roommates, asking one another questions over dinner, a sort of game, and the answers evolved into lists:

- Best desserts when the temperature gets above 70 degrees (ice cream, of course, but also frozen grapes).
- Three best books of all time (and why).
- The most unreasonable requests at work or school.

The questions grew more and more sophisticated. Flo treated Teddy like an adult, and in any case Teddy never seemed to enjoy the things her peers loved: the slumber parties, the shirts beaming with sequins in the shape of peace signs. The other girls had seemed silly, before they were mean. Flo and Teddy had each other; they were together in all this.

"Our schedule is pretty free-form when Justin is away," Taylor says. "Sometimes we have breakfast for dinner!" She laughs, wearily. "I tell Judah we're having an adventure. And then I make myself a cocktail!"

"Yep," Flo agrees. "I've been there myself."

Flo had certainly thought their flight to Florida would be an adventure; didn't everyone long to live near the beach? When Flo woke each morning in Tallahassee, for a while at least, she felt a jolt of gladness.

"Judah seems to be having fun," Flo observes. "Hey, I wanted to ask—"

"Yeah, he's pretty easy," Taylor agrees.

"My daughter was easy at that age."

But then Teddy grew up, didn't she? And she had disliked everything about Florida that recommended it to most others. Her fair tallowy skin burned in the sun. Orange juice gave her a sour stomach. And the sole time they went to Disney World, they waited in lines so long that by mid-afternoon Teddy asked if they could go home. The choice Flo had made for them both turned out to serve only herself, and only for a while—because if it didn't serve her child it served no one. Right? Is that what she's learned, after all?

It wasn't that Flo believed in Happily Ever After. In this way, she was like her mother. But she could feature, or at least hope for, a sort of Happily For A While. She kept trying—probably for too long—to make Florida a good place for herself and for Teddy, too.

"We used to live in Florida," Flo surprises herself by saying. "I liked it there, well, I liked being a student again, but my daughter didn't. It wasn't her dish of stew. So we moved."

"Yeah, we do that," Taylor says, and her voice is thoughtful. "We do that, don't we? We move, we adapt."

Flo laughs. "Yeah. I even left behind a guy. Who knows what would have happened if we'd stayed down there? I miss him. I mean, sometimes I do."

It was true. Flo *had* left behind a man, a work colleague who was a friend and might have turned into something more. He had been kind to Teddy on the few occasions when he'd come over for dinner, giving the child a bracelet made of braided cord that Teddy left behind when she packed for their move to the Midwest. Flo rescued that as she rescued other things of Teddy's: the soft bear with the caved face, and a pillowcase Flo had decorated for her daughter the year Teddy turned five. The smiling suns were brushed onto the pillowcase in thick fabric paint; this was one of the few times Flo tried to be "crafty."

Flo herself had, for a long time, believed in the simple sweetness of those smiling suns. But there was so much she couldn't control:

- Teddy's aloneness.
- The winters Teddy endured, literally and otherwise.
- The casual cruelty of the girls at Teddy's school(s).

"I miss my husband when he's out of town. But I do okay." Taylor swipes at some dust on the knee of her jeans. "*We* do okay," she amends.

"We do." Flo wonders how she would feel if Teddy decided to dislike *this* place, this desert where Flo has elected to stay. Should she ask her daughter not to come, after all?

"Does your daughter live here with you?"

"*No,*" Flo says. She stops, flustered. "But I've got some animal friends now."

Because this much was true: there hadn't been animals in Florida. Just plushies. The animals, the real ones, came later.

41

They stopped when night fell, the creature falling to its knees exhausted, and Ksenia exhausted also. They slept on a rocky ledge surrounded by the aspens in their golden cloaks, and the creature's dark rough fur provided warmth enough for them both.

"Are you even real?" Ksenia asked sleepily. She had wound her arms as far around his middle as they could go; it was like hugging a bear.

"I am," the creature said, and she trusted him. She felt less alone. The next morning Ksenia woke first, refreshed from her sleep, and hard as this world was, she was glad enough to wake in it.

42

Flo used to want Teddy to wake each day filled with hope. She wants this, still.

"So you have pets?" Taylor asks. She stretches, there on the bench, unselfconscious. Her shirt rides up and her belly is soft, pierced at the navel.

"Yes," Flo says. *Yes.*

This was the time.

"I'm looking for my dog, in fact. He's yea big." Holding her hand a distance from the ground. "With triangle ears? Have you seen him?"

"No, no dog today, but what's its name? In case I see it?"

"Dog," Flo says.

"Just Dog?" Taylor smiles. "I'll keep a lookout, okay?"

"Thanks. He's my cat's best friend and . . ." Flo trails off. It's maybe too hard to explain what Dog means to SilverGirl. What SilverGirl means to Flo. What all the animals' unconditional love means to Flo.

"Dog is very important," she says. "Sometimes I think I understand animal behavior better than human behavior."

"Uh-huh. You got *that* right!" Taylor laughs.

There was the time Teddy came home from school, her nose bloodied, some of the blood soaked into her denim jacket. Blood so proud, it never came out completely, though Flo scrubbed and scrubbed. This was in Florida. Teddy wouldn't say who had done it, though Flo had an idea. Teddy's nose wasn't broken and the school didn't help any, though years later Flo heard that the girl she thought was probably responsible had never left that town, had married early, and poorly, and Flo tried not to take satisfaction in this.

"It's okay," Flo would tell Teddy. "I love you." Outside, the palm fronds rattled. Flo kept a calendar in the kitchen and each night, except on holidays or weekends, they'd use a thick red marker to cross off the day that had come before. "See?" Flo would say. "One more down."

They were getting closer, they were counting down to something. They just didn't know what.

43

In the first powdered light Ksenia saw how the scales of the creature's hide had spread during the night, with dark fissures growing in the connecting places. Sleeping against the creature's flank, she had scratched her cheek on one of these knifelike scales. You will find what you need, her mother had said, and without thinking Ksenia rubbed the bit of blood from her cheek. She used her staff to mix the blood with the butter, which was, miraculously, still cool in its waxed wrappings. She made a smooth pink paste of this. While the creature slept on, she cleaned his scales with the vinegar her mother had packed. She used a shell from her pocket to scoop up gobbets of the paste, which she levelled into the fissures. She meant to soften the scales, to bring him some relief.

The creature had been sleeping with all three eyes closed, but now his brilliant third eye opened and he gazed upon her with tenderness. "Hello," Ksenia whispered.

She was hungry; she had used up her bread and the butter. And it was as if he knew, for the creature said, "There's food in my left ear," where Ksenia to her wonder found cakes, pink-sparkled, her favorite, which she ate. She was also thirsty, because she had given away the beer. The creature said, "There's drink enough in my right ear," and indeed there was wine, hidden in a pouch, so Ksenia drank. Fortified, she climbed onto the creature's back, and they continued on.

44

"THANKS FOR KEEPING an eye out for Dog." Flo stands. She watches Judah, who is running around the rubber pour, pretending to fly. "Have fun, you two. You are a good mother," she says sincerely.

"Oh! I bet you are, too!"

Flo smiles. She pats her pocket; Dog is out there somewhere, waiting to be found. But loneliness, it is a hunger. "You know, it's funny, I just heard from my daughter."

Taylor nods.

"She sent me a letter." Flo pulls the goat card out. It's hot, here in the park. There are no trees. Her ankle burns, and Teddy's card of course burns also. Flo opens it.

"When I was growing up, I didn't always like you," the next lines say.

Flo takes a breath. "She says I'm her role model."

Liar. Again.

Now this is the way it really was: at the end of the Florida time, Teddy started to withdraw. They moved to Ephrem, where Flo once had some family, though she didn't anymore, and at first Flo was hopeful. Teddy even made a friend. Darlene something, with the horrible brother Austin. But something was changing between them, between Teddy and Flo. They still watched television together; there were flashes of the old shared joys. Flo still bought packs of cupcakes in carnival colors; crumbs glittered on the floor. But in some ways they were no longer in sync. The stories Flo used to tell Teddy, for example, the ones she'd gotten from her own mother and the ones she made up—it was clear Teddy wasn't interested anymore.

Flo pretended she didn't notice how embarrassed Teddy was when Darlene came over: Flo with her cigarettes, her yellowed feet as tough as horn. It hadn't occurred to her until it was too late that there are certain things your children just don't want to see.

This hurt her feelings, but on some level Flo also understood. Flo didn't always like Teddy, either. Still, it was an effort, sometimes, to hide her feelings of loss.

- I know.
- I know.
- I know.

Flo repeats these words to herself now. Who can ever really know, exactly? But there is comfort in the words, in the idea of someone out there, even if it's just you, trying to understand.

"That's so sweet," Taylor says.

"I know." Judah has come to lean against his mother, and Taylor squeezes his shoulder. "We're very close," Flo adds. "My daughter, she and I used to do everything together. We still talk all the time."

"You've done a good job, then. Thanks for showing me how—I don't know, all the days and nights, it's worth it?"

"It gets easier," Flo lies—yet again! She feels almost giddy.

A phone rings then, some snippet of bright song, and Taylor pulls a cell phone out of her jeans pocket. "It's Justin!" she exclaims, beaming. She doesn't look quite so tired. Smiling at Flo, she holds the phone close to her ear.

"Hi, honey!" she exclaims. Her brow furrows, listening. "The reception's not so good here," she says. "Lemme move up a hill, see if that's better."

"Daddy! Daddy!" Judah cries. He jumps around his mother, reaching for the phone.

"Judah, sweetheart, let Mommy talk." Taylor looks at Flo, makes an *I'm sorry* face. "Listen," she says. "If I go up this hill"—Taylor points at a slope behind the climbing gym—"would you just keep an eye on Judah for a minute? Justin and I have been trying to reach each other all day! I'll stay where you can see me."

"Well, I—"

"I know it's a lot to ask, but it would mean so much!"

"Oh hon, I'm not—"

"You're a parent; you know how it is. Remember? We moms help each other out!" Taylor's smile is beseeching. "His work schedule is so crazy, it's hard to connect." She tucks her phone between her shoulder and ear, she makes a heart with her hands. "I'll help you find your Dog after, I swear! Thanks so much!" Taylor stands and pushes the backpack next to Flo. "Just give him a snack and I'll be right back!" She starts moving sideways up the incline, Judah at her hip. "Judah!" Taylor says. "You stay right here. Mind Miss Teddy now! I'll be right up the hill."

"I wanna talk to Daddy!" Judah cries. "Hi, Dadeeeeee! Daddy, hi!"

Taylor extricates herself from Judah's grip and moves quickly away.

"She'll be right back," Flo says, but Judah just watches Taylor climb the hill.

"Mama!" Judah says. Flo hears him, but Taylor doesn't.

Flo watches the boy anxiously. It's been a long time since she's been alone with someone else's child. With any child.

Judah comes slowly back to the rubber pour and plunks down, his face transformed by a scowl.

"Do you want a snack?" Flo asks him. She pats the bench next to her.

"No," the boy says, but he gets up and moves nearer, dragging his feet. "Where's my mom going?"

"She's just talking to your dad on the phone. We can still see her; look!" Flo points up the incline; Taylor looks tiny, way up on the hill like that, but then she turns and waves. Flo waves back; Judah, next to the bench now, crosses his arms and frowns.

"It's okay, hon," Flo says, and Judah gives her a black look.

"Don't call me hon!"

"Okay, okay. You want some . . . crackers, *Judah*?" Flo, surprised by the sudden edge in her voice—why is she saddled with someone else's kid?—digs in the backpack Taylor left on the bench. She extracts another baggie of crackers and a Thermos. "You want something to drink?"

"I'm not 'spose to take food from strangers."

"This is from your mom's bag—" Flo begins, but then, suddenly exhausted, she shrugs. "Suit yourself."

Judah moves away from her, and the two of them watch Taylor on the hill. She's talking animatedly now, waving her arms happily.

"I don't like you," Judah says suddenly. "Your shoes are ugly."

Flo sighs. Before Teddy did what she did, she was nicer—*easier* than other children. Flo doesn't know how to talk to a typical kid. She never did. Whatever else Teddy was, or is, she's never been . . . *that*.

Flo settles on another shrug. "I like them," she says.

"You're old like my grandma." Judah's bottom lip is thrust out now. "I bet you can't do this." He does a somersault then, right on the rubber pour.

Flo laughs in spite of herself. Hell, she'll show the little brat. "I actually can," she says. Slipping out of her plastic sandals, she crouches on the ground, favoring the bad ankle, and executes one awkward flip. "See?"

Judah almost grins. "Again!" he says, and does another somersault.

Flo complies, but this time her head spins a little and she lands on her ass.

Judah seems satisfied, though. "Can you do this?" He leaps up and climbs a ramp that leads to a tube slide.

"Sure," Flo says. She follows him up to the platform. "You going down the slide?" She looks up at Taylor. She's still there. Still talking.

"No! This!" Judah jumps to the ground, landing on all fours, like a cat.

"Hmmmm," Flo says. "Maybe." The platform isn't too far up; she figures she can land on her good foot, and without pausing to think it through, takes the leap. She lands on her good foot, but a little shock goes through the bad ankle, too.

"How about this?" Judah, smiling now, is already up the ramp again. A little ladder leads to a higher platform and the boy scales it quickly. "Can you jump from here?"

"Too rich for my blood," Flo says, laughing. "Come on down."

"No," Judah says. "I'm a big boy."

Flo looks up the incline again at Taylor, who is halfway turned, not paying attention, still talking enthusiastically. Flo waves, tries to get her attention. "Judah, come down now," she says. She keeps the tone friendly.

"You're not my mother."

Flo takes a breath. "Your mom wouldn't want you to jump." She feels the old anger, stirring, but knows to keep it out of her voice; she's got this.

"I'm a big boy," Judah repeats. "See?"

It takes seconds. Flo, forgetting her ankle, runs up the ramp. "Stop!" But Judah's already jumped, and when he flails midair and lands on his side, he screams. Without thinking, Flo jumps off the lower platform again; this time she lands on both feet and the pain in the bad ankle is excruciating.

"God*damn*it!" she cries. She limp-runs over to where Judah is lying on his back, howling.

"You're okay," she says, because she wants that to be so.

"Mamaaaaa!" Judah screams.

Taylor's definitely paying attention now. It's amazing, in fact, how quickly she makes it down the hill. "I've got to go!" she yells into the phone. Then, to Flo: "I asked you to watch him for *one* minute!" Her face is asymmetrical with fear and anger.

"I told him not to jump!"

Taylor pushes Flo aside and gathers Judah into her arms. "You okay, baby?"

"I wanna go home!" Judah cries. "I don't like her!" He points at Flo with one chubby baby finger.

Taylor murmurs into his hair, then turns to Flo accusingly. "I thought you said you had kids!"

"I did! I *do*! It was an accident. Accidents happen! No one died!" Flo backs up, wincing at the pain in her ankle. If she was angry before, she's just panicked now. What if the kid broke his back?

Taylor turns away from her and helps Judah stand up. "What hurts?" she asks her son. She's using a saccharine baby voice and suddenly Flo hates her, Taylor of the soft middle and dirty hair. Flo hates Taylor and she hates the woman's ordinary, entitled son.

"Move your head," Taylor says in that baby voice. "Move your arms, lovey." She has Judah lift up one leg, then the other. "Can you walk okay?"

"Can we get ice cream?"

"Anything you want, sweetheart."

"See, he's fine," Flo says. Taylor, scooping up the backpack, turns with a glare. "No wonder your dog's missing," she says. "And he needs a fucking *name*." She and the miraculously whole Judah flounce past. Flo scoffs but the woman's words sear. She pushes her feet back into her sandals. She loves them, still. Her shoes. Her happy red shoes.

People come and go. Already Flo misses what might have been. It's like a phantom limb: how she and this Taylor might have helped one another.

Did she really think that Taylor could save her?

Flo watches their retreating backs. Judah is skipping now, no doubt talking about ice cream, about chocolate and vanilla. Strawberry. *The little jerk is fine*, Flo thinks bitterly. *He needs to grow a pair.* ("It's not what you think but what you do about it," Sunby says in her head.)

"I didn't lose my temper," Flo tells Taylor and Judah as they move farther and farther away.

They don't hear her, of course.

"I didn't lose my temper," she reminds herself.

Flo hobbles away from the park, conscious of the time that has passed. She should have left sooner! She deserves what she gets!

Guilt being her constant companion. *Dog.* What if she no longer has a dog? Flo rakes at the eczema. She is going to The Place.

Her ankle screams.

45

Flo and Teddy had left California together. They left Florida together, still a proper family in Flo's estimation. But Teddy was to leave Ephrem on her own. Juvie was in the south and west of the state, and Teddy lived there until she turned 21. After Flo followed her there, to JuvieLand, she remained until Teddy got out, and then even for a little bit beyond that.

But there had been a moment for Flo, driving out of Ephrem to be near Teddy. For just that moment Flo thought she would turn her car in a completely different direction: east, maybe. She imagined just driving, gloriously alone. She imagined the Atlantic Ocean, shining like dulled silver. Waiting for her.

Flo didn't do that, though. No one, not even Sunby, understood how much courage that took.

PART TWO

46

They came to a great river that was so wide at one place it looked like a sea. Ksenia had never seen the like.

The river was called Seolfor, and on this side of it, an old woman shook her fist and screeched at their approach, "Who scares my rabbits and game? What creature is this, with the hooves of a beast and the speed of a raptor?"

47

In Ephrem, they were outsiders, even before the incident. Flo felt this. Teddy certainly did. Everyone needs to feel at home in the world.

Here in the desert, Flo and Dog have felt at home in The Place. Flo pictures him there now, perhaps listening to the river as they often do together. Flo sometimes wonders if the river will speak to her and her alone. She is patient. She has time.

Today, not so much, she reminds herself.

But listen: Dog will be there today, and he will not be alone, and none of it will be the way Flo imagines. Just like motherhood. Just like life.

Perhaps she will be rewarded. Maybe she won't.

But she's not there yet, she's not afraid yet, and the sun, it pours down.

48

The creature pulled up short so that Ksenia had to grip his horns tight to keep her seat, to keep from flying headlong. The old woman came closer, and it was as though she glided across the ground. She was a witch, her hair worn in great disarranged bunches around her head, and on her back slantwise hung a blackthorn cudgel. She smiled then, at the creature and Ksenia. But when she spoke her breath was hot and smelled like shit. (Had Flo's mother really said **shit***? Flo sometimes wondered. Perhaps it was offal.) Her breath smelled like offal, and rotted meat, and in this way Ksenia knew the danger.*

The creature shifted so that Ksenia might slide from his back, and then he reared up on his haunches and he was at his full height: two men tall. "Go from here," the creature said to Ksenia, "and wait for me at the round rock in the forest clearing. I must fight this witch, and if I win you will know it because the world will turn blue as my eye. Wait for me then, and do not leave the rock for your own safety's sake."

"Blue," Ksenia said, and she was afraid, but the creature turned from her. The hag was waiting. The two of them began their contest, circling and feinting, and the power they displayed was a terrible thing to see.

Ksenia fled.

49

Good and evil. Within others. Within ourselves. Teddy was at least as good as Flo herself was. Probably better, Flo thinks. Flo hopes.

After all, Flo reminds herself: the name Theodora meant God's gift. Teddy's full name had been Flo's idea; even at the time she felt it might cover all the bases. Make up for Flo's own flaws, and Charlie's. The ones Teddy hadn't yet discovered in herself.

50

Flo puts stock in naming things, and sometimes you just know.

That car, for example. Flo, walking slowly to favor her ankle, passes a Mustang painted the most delirious shade of green. You are Fancy, Flo decides.

Another car, this one black as pitch, is Gallows. Of course. It was obvious.

The same could be said for SilverGirl's name, which just declared itself. The cat required the exact right name, having saved Flo (the cat did save her); Flo loves every animal but SilverGirl will always be special because of this. The tabby will eventually live past 20 despite a pronounced limp and, at the end, a shortage of teeth. But Flo doesn't know this yet. What she knows is that she and SilverGirl watch television together. Now Dog watches with them, he and the cat are inseparable, but at the beginning it was just the two of them, Flo and SilverGirl.

This started when Teddy was in Juvie. Flo didn't have any friends in that town, though she liked it that way. She didn't have friends because people didn't know her, which was different from the way things had been in Ephrem, where she didn't have friends because people thought they knew her. Flo realized with a jolt that she was happy alone, which went against the grain of everything she'd been told growing up.

"You are Alone," Flo tells a third car, a two-seater with a missing taillight.

And SilverGirl was all she needed, during a time when Flo needed everything. Pressing her face against the firm rich round of the cat's flank, Flo would breathe SilverGirl in. The cat smelled like warm things—Fritos, worn leather—

and Flo would burrow her face and feel her soul expand. She felt more human, actually.

During this time Flo was almost happy; to be unknown was sweet, like jelly in the mouth. Because people could be strange. During her life, during her career as a social worker, Flo had heard the most extraordinary things. She always thought she couldn't be surprised anymore and then someone went ahead and told her something else.

Of course Flo's whole life has been one surprise after another. Hasn't it?

Near the park is a pet store. On their walks to The Place, Flo and Dog will stop here. They look in the windows together because sometimes animals lounge there: the great tortoise with its rumpled gorget, and usually cats. Dog, who likes most other animals, smiles at them. Flo is pretty sure they smile back.

Perhaps Dog came here today. Without her.

Flo came here once alone, when SilverGirl was sick. The woman who runs this place is a middle-aged divorcee with a propensity for tank tops and a starved look about her, except for the skin under her arms, which wiggles. (And was that a wart on her nose?) Ugly but kind, she dispenses advice about pets the way a vet would, but for free.

Christmas before last, Flo brought a poinsettia back to the apartment, from The Mutiny. In the sap of the poinsettia are chemicals: diterpenoid euphorbol esters, and saponin-like detergents.

Flo found this out later. She hadn't known anything about poinsettias when she bought that one, and neither had SilverGirl, who ate some of the flower; the milky-white sap made her drool.

It was Dog who noticed something was wrong. Flo, just home from work, had cracked a beer, but Dog refused to settle; he paced and whined. He wouldn't let her be. Flo thought he needed to go out but he led her into the bedroom, where SilverGirl had taken refuge in the closet. Crouching just outside the door, Dog bared his teeth and cried. He understood SilverGirl. He understood fear.

So did the woman at the pet shop, who also knew something about poinsettias. Don't be afraid, it was all right, she told Flo. The cat would be okay.

"Can I give her something to feel better?" Flo remembers asking.

"Aw honey, just give her your lap." The pet shop woman touched Flo's arm. She had tiny wrists, like a child.

Flo went back to the apartment. She wrapped SilverGirl in her arms and sat with her and Dog, watching television, till the worst of it was over. Dog wouldn't leave SilverGirl's side; when Flo got up to heat some dinner, Dog clambered into the chair with the cat, he curled himself around her. SilverGirl licked her lips, again and again, but the pet shop woman was right: she was okay.

"Poor SilverGirl, she's been to battle," Flo told Sunby later on the phone. "We dodged a bullet. Dog knew," she added. "Dog is my hero."

What she didn't say was how the incident reminded her of the way things can be fine and then go sideways in an instant. For example. Even as they talked, cancer was burrowing like a mealworm through Sunby. Carving him up. Although no one knew it, not yet.

They'd all find out soon enough. But at that point what Flo did was tell Sunby what he already knew: how living in JuvieLand, Flo hadn't minded being alone. But how she would have been lonely without SilverGirl, who appeared one day, taking up residence in Flo's parking stall. "That's how we met," Flo reminded Sunby. "It started with the bits of chicken I took her. And the plastic dish of water." Eventually Flo had left her patio door slatted open—she was on the first floor, she always lives on the first floor if possible—and SilverGirl just moved right in. "She had fleas, but I took care of that," Flo said.

Sunby, who had heard SilverGirl's origin story countless times, did what he did so well: he listened. He also showed concern about SilverGirl's health scare, but not too much concern, not enough to make things worse. "Do you think she lost some weight, at least?" he asked, to make Flo laugh. She could picture his joking face. They both knew SilverGirl was pretty chonk—eighteen pounds or thereabouts—because Flo weighs the cat occasionally, using a suitcase scale. Sunby could joke because they both knew SilverGirl was going to be okay. "Oh yeah, I'm sure she has," Flo said.

The weight didn't stay off. SilverGirl has a body dense as a haystack. She brings Flo mice and then proceeds to eat them unless Flo acts quickly enough and disposes of the body: every organ, every bone, nothing is wasted. Flo is no longer mortified by this. It is SilverGirl's way. And the cat remains a reassuring pressure on Flo's lap when they watch television together. With Dog, of course. There was one show, a miniseries about Chernobyl. It was disturbing, the duplicity and politicking and the horrible ways people died.

But there was nobility in there, too. People who acted with conscience and grace. See, there was always both, Flo told the animals. She rubbed her knuckles against the top of Dog's head, she stroked the cat's massive back. SilverGirl's coat was short and smooth. It felt like greasy velvet, and her bulk was such that her fur folded and rippled under Flo's hand. "I know," Flo reassured them as the images unfolded, one after another. The red smokestacks. The red faces. "I know."

Dog isn't here, Flo can see that, but she limps over and presses her face against the glass windows of the pet store. No tortoise today. No cats. Hi, Flo thinks to the empty windowfronts, because the animals are in there somewhere. She considers going in, asking about Dog and buying him a bone. Or a toy. An act of hope, for when they are together again. But when she tries the door it's locked; the divorcee keeps random hours, she's told Flo she has another job, something with accounting.

"Damn." It occurs to Flo then: she would miss Dog as much as SilverGirl would.

Which is saying something.

Gods, Flo thinks. Sometimes she surprises herself.

The summers were longer when Flo was a girl. And when her daughter was young. Everything seemed very clear: this is right, this is wrong. The days are paler, flatter now. Their nuances are bewildering. Maybe this is aging. Flo doesn't know, though maybe Sunby would have.

She could tell him things. "I'm tired," she could say. "I'm afraid." Or, "A part of me is very old." And Sunby would understand that she was talking about her heart.

51

Clutching her staff, Ksenia ran from that place, into the wildwood beside the great river. She ran until she reached the clearing, where a round rock was set into the earth's crust like a gem. She climbed its smooth surface and waited at the top for what seemed a day, or three, and during this time the earth around her became clear and rippling, as if Ksenia floated in a great sea. After a time that rippling transparency became blue and bright, and even the trees ringing the clearing shone indigo, wonderful and terrible both. And such was Ksenia's astonishment that in this moment she forgot what the creature had said to her and she leapt from the rock. Thinking not of grace, nor of the creature. Thinking not of her mother. Thinking only to flee.

(This was always the part little Flo hoped would change, but it never did. As much as Flo's mother embellished and embroidered the story over the years, this part was always the same. "What if she stayed on the rock, just this once?" Flo might ask. "But she doesn't," her mother would say. Then, seeing Flo's face: "Don't blame her. We're all afraid of what we don't understand.")

52

TEDDY. WHEN SHE was first out of Juvie, her quiet despair could take up all of the air in a room.

"Do I frighten you?" Teddy asked Flo once, during that time.

"No, you're funny!" Flo lied.

Flo turns from the pet store, sucking at her teeth. When Nell called and told her that Sunby had died, Flo sucked air through her teeth, again and again. "No one told me," Flo finally said, although Nell was telling her.

When Flo's mother was dying, a priest would come to her bedside; his voice got softer and softer with each visit. He didn't know Flo; he barely knew Flo's mother. Flo wasn't sure if the visits brought comfort to her mother, who told her daughter once, near the end, "The dance is over, put the guitar back in the case."

And after Flo's mother died, that part of Flo's life—being an earthbound daughter—was over. Flo had already left Charlie behind. Being Teddy's mother was a comfort to her, then.

Flo herself does not pray in a conventional sense, but: "I still talk to my mother," she told Sunby once. This was some time after her mother's death. Flo had these one-sided conversations mostly when she was very sad. Sunby, who did pray, of course, told Flo that talking to her mother was prayer enough.

Enough for what? She liked Sunby too much to ask.

Flo's neck feels raw, open. On days like this she has to be especially careful. She wants to scratch. She tries not to.

She has to be careful with Teddy, too, prickly as she is. Their relationship being different than the one Flo shared with her own mother.

After Teddy got out of Juvie she was sensitive in a new, profound way. Flo suspected—no, she knew—that Teddy was cutting at her arms. Flo said nothing. Not because she didn't care. She cared. But she and her daughter were trying to get to know one another again; saying anything would surely make things worse. At least that's what Flo thought. Whatever she'd learned about being a social worker, it seemed unrelated to the raw troughs on Teddy's arms.

Those case studies she'd pored over in school! The papers she'd written! *Do this, and this,* she'd asserted, and the professors rewarded her with As. Real life, of course, being an entirely different beast. The one and only time Flo sat Teddy down and tried to practice what she thought she knew—what a joke! *Cringe,* as Teddy herself might have said.

"Don't try out your social work on me," is what Teddy *did* say, flatly, and Flo never did, after that exchange. Her education proved to be inadequate when it came to her daughter, and Flo decided that her role, at least for a while, was simply to keep Teddy fed. Even on those days when Teddy wouldn't eat. She wasn't hungry, she said, she was afraid. So Flo was, too.

Sometimes Teddy said nothing. Sometimes she would speak deliberately, as if Flo were slow, or as if Teddy herself were in a show. Her smiles were rare, almost professional. Flo, who could no longer hear what went on in her daughter's heart (if she ever had), suspected that Teddy was like the politest of guests, not saying everything she thought. And so Flo watched carefully, wanting to believe that Teddy was not a danger to others. Not anymore. She was less certain that Teddy was not a danger to herself; Flo sustained herself during these times by remembering Teddy was strong. That even weak things can survive and Teddy had the steel in her. Flo wanted to think her daughter, in her silence, was saving up energy for whatever came next.

And Flo herself is strong, isn't she? Just look at the way she's walking on this ankle! Any moment she'll see Dog. Maybe he has found ripe delicious garbage to roll in (though he's not really that kind of dog). Well then: maybe he is taking a long and secret nap.

Teddy always slept tucked up, like a cat. If she'd had a tail it would have been wrapped around her.

Flo's red sandals scrape the pavement and the sun is a weight.

She thinks about a place she visited once called Barking Sands. This was because when you walked on the beach, it made a strange barking sound. This phenomenon alarmed some people; Flo liked it.

When she finds Dog she will rename him:

- Barking Sand.

No. Not quite right.

Maybe:

- Red (because he is).
- Blue.

There is no wind. A kip of clouds stacks along the west horizon; Flo knows they will not make it this far.

Sometimes it seems to her that she has lived in the desert forever.

53

The next thing Ksenia heard was the hag, laughing. The woods were restored to what they had been but not exactly: now the witch was there also. She appeared before Ksenia, still cackling. "You must live and serve me," she said, gripping her blackthorn stick, and Ksenia remembered the creature's warning: do not leave the rock, for your own safety's sake. She heard the creature wailing for her, and Ksenia cried back to him, but she did not know if she could be heard. The forest belonged to the witch now, and Ksenia's voice was muffled, no matter how she cried.

Her mother had said: be in this world, not of it.

Too late.

54

After Teddy got out of Juvie, she moved into the apartment where Flo had been living during the years of Teddy's detention (Flo called it detention); she stayed during the height of COVID, they rode it out together. "I've graduated," Teddy declared after the COVID vaccine came out. In life? From the facility? To what? Flo never asked. But she would look into her daughter's troubled face and think: you're really smart. There was still that, that hadn't changed.

Then when Sunby helped Teddy get a job, up in Lead Grove, in northern Illinois near Ephrem, Flo was restless. There was no longer any reason to be where she was, although she remained in JuvieLand for the few months Teddy worked the factory job Sunby had found for her. On some level Flo was waiting for something to happen, and something did: Teddy left Lead Grove, and Flo felt she could just pack up and leave then, too. JuvieLand, sure, but also Illinois. She took SilverGirl, she took a few special items. She told her landlord he could have the rest. Even the unopened ice cream in the freezer; even the couch Flo had salvaged, with its SilverGirl-shaped indents.

She picked up odd jobs on the road, living out of her car, staying over in Walmart parking lots. She didn't shower every day; she still doesn't. During this time, people had contradictory ideas about COVID, and Flo heard them all. In some states, there were mandatory mask policies; in others there weren't.

Flo herself donned many masks.

Filling up her car at a gas station in West Virginia (she finally made it east!), where the hills folded like a sheet, again and again, she was Sally. Sally was hardy and silent.

At a diner in the Middle West, she was Hilary, joking with her waitress and carefree. She tried on these roles like sweaters, then moved on. This was liberating in its way. Also liberating: the sense that disaster had stolen, but also freed her of her old life, of old expectations and constraints. How comparatively easy it had been for her to roll away from it all. For a while, anyway.

If she retained few possessions during this time, she has started to accrue things here in the desert. Including memories. Maybe especially memories. Things have a way of doing that, of catching up with you.

We make choices, again and again and again.

Something she has always brought along, no matter where she lived: an old baby doll. It has been Flo's since the age of eight. In those days, eight wasn't too old for a baby doll, though Flo suspects that's different now. The doll was probably the nicest gift Flo ever received; it was a Madame Alexander doll, and even then Flo understood that her mother probably couldn't afford it. She also knew that her mother found the doll to be beautiful, and trusted Flo to have this beautiful thing.

The doll came with the name Pussycat, which had sounded perfectly natural then, and which Flo reverently kept. Pussycat also came with a knit sweater, footie pajamas, a dress for everyday, and a dress for special. Flo was a careful child, and the doll remains in good condition. After Teddy came along, she played with Pussycat, a little. But she did not love her as Flo does, and there is a sorrow there, and probably a lesson: how something can be so important, and then not.

Flo has kept the doll.

She can't go back to who she was as a little girl. And Teddy was, ultimately, a different kind of little girl.

Once, Flo stopped at a town with a clean bright YMCA. This was somewhere in the Plains, in a snowstorm. She had planned to sleep in her car that night but the weather was too risky. She found a motel room, but its bathroom stank so of bleach and mildew that she went to the local Y to shower and to swim. The young woman at the motel's front desk had assured her the pool would be open; COVID was at the point where some pools were. Her pink swimsuit wasn't too loose then, and at the pool she had one lane to herself. In a corner a gaggle of old women wore masks with their rubber petal swim caps and skirted suits; they complained about how cold it was, and Flo, she loved their raucous bitching. The other lanes were occupied by members of the local firefighting crew, who practiced water rescues using a floating plastic platform meant to represent a shelf of ice.

It was remarkable, Flo thought, watching the crew, to have such purpose. The firefighters wore heavy suits with valves that expelled the extra air. Weights around their ankles kept them upright. In that moment, Flo wished such a thing existed for navigating life. Wouldn't that be something, she said to one of the firefighters, a young man with cropped dark hair who nodded shyly. Sure it would, he said.

Sunby would say our faith keeps us upright. But it could also be an anchor. Flo thought about that as she swam: just breaststroke, that's all she knows. She is not an elegant swimmer. But she frog-kicked for a full hour that night in the clean bright water and felt like a normal person, a community member. It was easy enough to pretend she fit in *here*. She didn't want to leave the pool.

She stayed for nearly a week in that town, even after the weather cleared. Flo drove to the Y every day, and in the pool there was no winter. Every day she'd use the same locker, #139. This was her routine. This was the world she had made.

After five days she knew she'd either have to find work or drive on. The motel charges added up. And they didn't really take pets, though SilverGirl was quiet and no one but Flo knew she was there. All night Flo dreamt of her, in fact, her solidity, and these dreams made Flo happy, though one night there was also a dream of a red dog wearing a pink collar. This dream made her happy also.

Flo was content here, in the motel on the Plains, but ultimately she found herself thinking about warmer climes. Melting snow tapped outside her window and the room was a furnace. It was time to go, but before she did she opened the windows, she opened drawers. In the nightstand she found:

- A ring set with a chunky blue stone.
- Two toothbrushes, still in their wrappers.
- A grimy stuffed animal, shaped like a whale.

This last made her a little sad. She took the ring and, on second thought, the toothbrushes.

She wears the ring now, doesn't she?

And life kept adding up. Sometimes fiercely. It's possible Flo has come to this strange arid place to slow it down. Dog, however, might have moved on. Like Teddy did, Flo thinks.

Flo pictures Dog's face. His eyes are expressive: brown with the gold lights in them. Like syrup. Like treacle. This is a good thing to remember and so he is alive, he must be.

There is no other way.

55

That first long night Ksenia could hear the creature, his calls for her unceasing. Ksenia's voice was still muffled by magic; all she could do was listen and silently weep. The animals of that place, simple forest folk, saw her pain, and though they feared the witch, they took pity on her, bringing pine branches and duff to cover Ksenia so that she might rest. When she finally slept, it was near dawn and her dreams were uneasy. The sun had hardly risen when Ksenia was awakened by the hag, who poked her with the length of blackthorn. Ksenia sat up, and the woods were silent.

The hag saw her listening, and laughed a laugh like three hundred rusted hinges and three thousand knocking engines. "He's gone," she said. "Did you think he would save you?"

56

It wasn't that Sunby's death was a surprise. He'd had the Whipple procedure and that bought him almost a year. It was a good year. He kept up with his ministry—no small feat, as churches everywhere were shrinking—and at the end he was taking care of two little congregations, traveling back and forth between them. Sunby and Nell also traveled: to Omaha to see a friend, and then to Japan of all places. Sunby wanted to ride the bullet train and he did. Then the pain in his gut returned. He was tired most of the time, and beer no longer tasted good to him. Sunby got a scan and the cancer was back. Such a good man and this was what his body had made: there were secondary tumors now, bundled deep into his liver.

Sunby and Nell called with the news. "I'll live through whatever's left," Sunby said, and Flo could hear the wonder in his voice. Nell had survived breast cancer earlier in their marriage, and it clearly hadn't occurred to Sunby, or to his wife, that he might not win this one. He wasn't a person who felt sorry for himself, though. He was calm.

Flo was calm, too; she is pretty sure she was kind. But in the days afterward she was depressed, and sometimes she told herself that the doctors were wrong, that it would all be okay. She needed Sunby too much for him to go and die on her.

And death was confusing, of course. Flo didn't always know what was going on with Sunby's treatment. As the disease grew, he often was too tired to talk on the phone. "He needs all his energy just to be," Nell told her once when Flo called. Nell wasn't impatient but she sounded exhausted too, and Flo didn't feel comfortable pressing her with questions about the chemotherapy, when and how often it would be.

Whether it was even still going on. How much time might be left. She was left to guess and do her best, which was something like parenting, she supposed, and so familiar in its way.

She and SilverGirl and Dog watched a lot of television. Sometimes Flo imagined that Teddy, a different Teddy, was watching with them and holding her hand.

She calls for Dog—well, now she's whistling really. Dog has always liked that, her whistle, which is sharp and clear; he's always come running.

Not today.

Gods I'm tired, Flo thinks.

At night when she can't sleep, Flo re-reads the letters she has gotten from Teddy. For a while Teddy would write to her in Derrykin. The letters were long, using words and phrases Flo had never learned or didn't remember, and she told her daughter to stop that, write in English and so Teddy did, but after that the letters were shorter and there weren't as many; they were hard to understand in their own way. Did Teddy *want* to be a puzzle?

But Flo always responded, writing letters by hand. Teddy moved so much, who knew if she got them?

Now there is this new card. Flo pauses. She will read one more line. Or a few.

"I guess in some ways Sunby was our go-between for a while. I miss him," Teddy writes. "I haven't heard from him lately."

When Nell called with the news of Sunby's death, Flo talked about the way she and Nell and Sunby would sit out on milk crates behind the storefront church where Sunby preached. This was when Flo was still living in Ephrem, but after what Teddy did. Not many people were willing to be Flo's friend anymore at this point, or at least admit to it publicly, but Sunby and Nell didn't seem to care what anyone else thought. The three of them would sit out there, in the bright throat of the sun, smoking cigarettes and just chopping it up; during these times their laughter was a promise that Flo would eventually get over it all. Sunby, who probably quit smoking three times during their friendship, would draw deeply on his cigarette and say things like, "We're making merry hell now, aren't we?" Flo herself hadn't quit yet, either. She probably smoked more than ever in those days.

Sometimes he'd even talk about God. God-talk usually bored or even irritated Flo, but coming from Sunby it was okay. She'd tell him what she thought God was not—

- Magical.
- Transformative.
- Answerer of prayers.

—and he'd come back with something along the lines of "Well, sure, anyone can say what God *isn't*."

"He never answered my prayers," Flo repeated. She was really stuck on that (she still might be). "Back when I still prayed."

"He's not a prayer ATM," Sunby would say. He didn't say this in a mean way. He'd say, "And who the hell really knows what God *is*?"

"But that's your *job*," Flo said, and Sunby laughed and lit a new cigarette from the one he had going. "Maybe God doesn't even want to be defined," he said, adding, when he saw her face, "But I can certainly try."

It was clear Nell didn't remember any of this, which meant of course that it was hardly helpful to her. Flo's feelings were almost hurt! Sharing with Nell was supposed to be a kindness, but it was as if Flo herself was speaking a different language.

Of course Nell was grieving. And she'd been through the mill, hadn't she? After Sunby got sick the second time, he disintegrated so quickly, though when it was happening it seemed like he died for a long time, just peeling away, layers and layers of him. This was the way Sunby's cancer went. He was well, and then he wasn't.

Flo wants juice. She'll feel better then, she always does.

"What's inevitable?" she used to joke with Sunby. "Taxes, sure," she'd say. "But sugar. Sugar should be inevitable."

"Don't forget death." That was Sunby. He wasn't afraid to have the last word.

57

On the way to the river there is a dead rock squirrel, looking different every time Flo passes. Flo was a witness to its death. At first after it died, the body was burst and upsetting. Meat-looking. Wrong. But it has since dried out and become curious, like a husk. Today it is just a dim pan of bones and skin; it has lost its power to shock.

Flo often sees rock squirrels on her walks. They are active in the morning, or late in the day—as Flo herself is. When Flo first came upon this one, it was still alive, although its leg was wrong, there was blood. It must have been hit by a car. She saw the creature in the street and when she drew closer it tried to drag itself away, frantic with terror. Flo walked past, but after less than a block she doubled back. The squirrel was still in the road; it hadn't gotten far. Shivering, it regarded her, baring its tiny wet teeth. Flo tried not to think of her daughter, of Mrs. Benedict, when she took a rock to the squirrel. Her choice was meant to be a mercy.

Flo feels hard inside when she looks at the remains now, but the animal was better off than it had been, in pain and fearful. The wet, the *dark*, of its eye! Rock squirrels are social creatures, Flo knows this. At least it didn't die alone.

Coyote. Truck. What if *Dog* died alone? Flo thinks this, then screws up her eyes, *un*thinking it.

"Stay positive," Flo used to counsel Teddy. "All things are resolved in time." She almost believed this herself. At least she wanted to.

Flo could take a different route to The Place, to avoid the squirrel, but she never does. She passes what is left of it. Every day there is a little bit less; surely the day will come when it is finally gone.

58

Ksenia's first task was to fetch water from the well. Because it was an enchanted well, and the witch gave her an enchanted vessel, the task was Sisyphean; half the water spilled from the pail each trip she made. Sometimes it disappeared entirely.

But Ksenia was resilient and the animals of the forest were with her. Over time, in fact, she would learn their language; this was a gift amidst her suffering. The animals encouraged Ksenia to persist at her tasks, and so she did. They also helped her to secret her hazel staff away, beneath a tile of turf near the well's lip. The hag did not know about the staff, and the animals guarded this secret.

59

Flo hears a high clear barking, not like Dog's, but still. There is that spark of hope.

She used to hope: The thing in Ephrem? The *incident*? That she would wake and it would be a dream. A nightmare, escaped.

Sunby would have said, hope is akin to faith.

Hope, and faith, and charity, Flo thinks, in time to the clack of her shoes on the pavement. She hefts the staff in her hand.

Come on. Come on, now.

The staff was a gift, it helps with her ankle. It does.

60

SUNBY WAS IN HOSPICE at the end, and he died at home: his death when it came was abrupt. In those last weeks she talked to him once, on the phone.

"Will my death be like yours?" she asked.

Sunby had always wanted a clear, orderly death, messy though he knew life could be.

"I don't know," Sunby said, and then, maybe because he sensed Flo's fear, they spoke of other things.

Flo is a crucible. The sun is charged, a lamp. What *does* frighten her? Everything? Does she burn or shine?

Dog used to rumble, *brrrt, brrrt, brrrt.* Once upon a time, Flo had thought mothering was something she was good at.

The courage it takes to love! Again and again and again.

Keep walking! (Flo does.) Think of something else! (Flo does.)

Her galley kitchen. Vivid green as a cartoon frog and Flo thinks, often, that she will paint the walls. And what color would she choose? Not white like this screaming concrete. Something soft, like a bun. Something light that will open up the walls of her space.

Flo makes plans, and sometimes, more often than not, she does not act on them. Flo doesn't know why this is so. She meant to paint the kitchen. She meant to give Dog a beautiful name. A real one.

Her toilet has a ring of grime in it. She cleans. The ring always reappears, a dark enchantment.

61

Ksenia brought water from the well, and she scoured a cauldron that at first remained filthy, no matter how hard she scrubbed. If she wasn't competent straightaway, she grew better at these tasks, until even the witch could find no complaint. Ksenia's mother had taught her to persevere.

The hag in her turn was cunning, bringing the girl a basket at each eventide. In the basket were:

- *Fish.*
- *Cress.*
- *Delicious-looking cakes, sparkly and pink and rich with cream.*

"Eat," the hag demanded. But Ksenia feared, rightly, that the cakes were bewitched, and she missed the creature terribly in any case. She missed her mother. Ksenia could hardly eat for sorrow, and so she pushed the cakes aside.

The hag would make a terrible commotion then, wailing and shrieking before slipping sideways through a rent in the air. In this way she disappeared, not returning until the next day when the whole thing began again. Ksenia did eat some of the fish, wrapped in the cress, because she had to eat something, though first she took the fish into the quiet of the woods and she rolled it hard, with her hazel stick, to squeeze out any bad magic. The animals? Of course they helped her in this.

62

Eventually Flo met people she trusted here, in this desert town: B. of course, and the landlord. That elderly man next door, with his thick skin and cigarettes, who never wears a shirt but possesses surprising strength in his shingled arms. He hardly speaks! But he helped Flo string up her Christmas lights.

And before Flo met any of these people, she was alone (except for SilverGirl, of course); if that sounds sad Flo might argue that this situation also rang with possibility.

For example. When she first moved here, and found her apartment, and began to fill it with things, one night she bought a sandwich roll at the gas station mart. She heated it up in the microwave—*her* microwave. She ate it from her plate, reading a mystery novel. The plate she'd gotten at Goodwill; it bore a willow pattern and made Flo think of her own mother. Flo had opened a tin of food for SilverGirl, and the cat had her own willow-patterned plate also.

They ate quietly, together. Looking around the apartment, a space she had created for herself, Flo felt pride move warmly through her. In that moment, just the living and eating and being seemed like victory.

The silence had been thrilling, her happiness a private happiness. Unconnected to anything outside this room.

There is an open culvert she walks along to get to The Place. It is concrete and usually there is a little snake of sour water in it, running along the bottom. Today it is dry, like the inside of a box. Flo smells car exhaust and burnt concrete. She smells sage and the color white.

She and Teddy would ask one another those questions over pizza—*Do colors have smells? What color are you?*—creating their lists while the TV kept watch. *What makes you cry?* was a favorite question also. This was a long time ago, the game a luxury for those who hadn't gotten too sad yet. Flo never held back, but she did sometimes have a glass of wine when they played. Or a Twinkie.

She had her hacks, Flo did.

The sun is higher now, caroming off the white culvert. If she had a cellphone, this is whom she would call:

- Teddy (if Teddy had a number).
- Sunby (Flo's phone would be magical).
- Her mother (ditto the magic).
- Dog (again with the magic!).
- SilverGirl (of course).
- B. (her best living friend who is human).

This is a longer list than usual. Gods the sun is hot!

Flo keeps moving, counting her steps.

When she was young, she aspired to certain things. She wanted to learn languages, three at least. She planned to travel abroad. She thought it was in her to grow into someone both assured and graceful.

And though Flo persevered, she was none of these things, she did none of these things. Except for the language she—well, Teddy, really—had created. The gift of Derrykin. And when she became a mother, none of the rest of it mattered, so certain Flo was that she'd found what she was meant to do.

Flo stops counting her steps.

Life is humbling. Parenthood is humbling. For a long time, Flo had looked younger than her age. People would comment on her youthfulness. Around the time of the troubles, this changed abruptly and forever. And now that she has stopped dyeing her hair, she figures she looks the way she will look for the rest of her life. More or less.

Every time Flo sees her daughter, Teddy looks the same but also different. There is always the fear that she won't recognize her daughter at all. This hasn't happened yet, although the changes can be significant.

One time, for example, Teddy was very thin. This was after she got out of Juvie and moved back to northern Illinois. She had always been slight but this was something new: her face pinched, shoulders pointed as wings. Flo, who was visiting, worried at first that her daughter had gotten into drugs, but it wasn't that. There was simply a nervous energy that could not be contained. Teddy drank a lot of coffee and her teeth were stained with it. Flo knew better than to mention this. All that short time that they were together, Teddy wore a baseball cap with the brim pulled low; Flo could not see her daughter's face. Just those brown teeth, and her lips so chapped and chewed. Teddy wore long sleeves, but Flo knew the scars were there.

They had met for lunch near but not in Ephrem. They met in Lead Grove, an industrial town with a handful of decent restaurants; this is where Sunby had found Teddy work, packing corn in a factory. Lead Grove was far enough away from Ephrem that Teddy figured she was unlikely to run into anyone she knew. And she needed the work.

"Do you want to change your name?" Flo had asked her daughter when Teddy accepted the job. Mrs. Benedict's death had gotten a lot of coverage; Teddy's name would have been at least vaguely familiar to anyone who watched the news.

"No," Teddy said. "I know who I am."

For three months, Teddy packed corn, and for three months she stayed with a friend of Nell's, because Flo was still living in the apartment back in JuvieLand. Flo hadn't decided where to go next, but she knew it wouldn't be Lead Grove. Too close to Ephrem. Flo knew her limits.

Nell's friend was kind enough. Teddy had her own room, she had Wi-Fi.

And so Flo drove up north to meet her daughter after Teddy got settled in. My God, she was nervous. Flo was. Even though she wasn't going to Ephrem. "It's probably PTSD," she told Sunby. Joking/not joking. She hadn't been back to the area, not even to visit Sunby. And in the end, it turned out living anywhere near Ephrem wasn't possible for Teddy either. What she'd done being like a stain that spread and spread.

Flo understood.

She taps her pocket lightly; she can feel the notecard through the fabric. "I keep on moving," the card says. "But when I get to the next place, I'm still the same."

For a long time, after the business with Mrs. Benedict, Flo thought that there was no getting better, or over, or through. But everything disappears, eventually. Every day she gets a little farther from it. Also, further.

The next moment, the next place, doesn't have to be worse. That's what Sunby always thought. That's what he said, after he knew he was dying, about wherever he is now.

A cloud becomes rain. On this earth at least it does.

When Teddy left the factory job, she called Flo, who still had a cellphone then, who still thought that was important. Flo suspected Sunby made Teddy call, but her daughter did call, there was that. "I felt like a kitchen bitch in that factory," Teddy said to Flo on the phone. This expression was something she had learned at Juvie and it amused her, she said. Flo knew that repeating it was her daughter's way of being brave. Or sounding brave. Teddy said that she was leaving Lead Grove that day—"I'm off to parts unknown"—and Flo thought, now we will both go out into the world.

There was a long silence. Some people were afraid of silence, they tried to fill those spaces with words, anything, even if there was nothing to say. But Flo and Teddy have never been that way. Flo waited, and then she said, "Do you remember the story about the seeker? Meeting the three workers?"

Teddy said she did.

Flo asked if Teddy wanted to hear it again and Teddy said yes, it had been a while, so yeah. Which surprised Flo a little but she went ahead.

"Okay then," Flo said. "Once upon a time, back in your grandma's time, there was a seeker. He was what some people call a pilgrim, traveling by foot, though there were cars then, of course there were. He was walking to a river, where the waters were rumored to be restorative. One of his legs was shorter than the other. He might have had polio as a child—who knows? But the going was hard."

"Is this true?" Teddy asked. "Or made up?" And in that moment it was almost like old times.

"Once something is made up, it's real enough, isn't it?" Flo said. She paused for just a moment, then continued, the way her own mother used to when Flo asked questions. "When he was almost to the river, he was passed by a caravan of three covered trucks. They passed him without stopping, dust rising in their wake, but in time the pilgrim—let's call him Joe—caught up with them. The trucks were all pulled up neatly, and the three drivers were having a smoke and talking and laughing. Joe limped up and asked how things went with them.

Things are bad, the first one said, shaking his head and flicking his cigarette into the road. I work 24/7, it's shit work, and I'll never get paid enough for what I do.

The second one said, There's not much work to be had, and I'm glad to get this. I'm not from here, he added. I send money to my family. He pronounced family like *fambly*, a detail Flo liked for some reason and always included.

The third one said, This is my life now. I'm building Hoover Dam.

Flo had probably heard this story from her own mother. Or some version of it.

"The Hoover Dam is a remarkable thing," Flo said. "Sometimes we're doing something amazing with our lives and we just can't see it."

There was a pause. "What happened to Joe?" Teddy finally asked. She had never asked this before.

"I don't know," Flo said. And after a pause she added quietly, "I don't think I can help you." Even as she said it she wished everything were different and she guessed, correctly, that Teddy would never mention this exchange (she hasn't). Flo also guessed, probably correctly, that neither of them would ever forget it.

She doesn't know where Teddy moved next; she didn't hear from her daughter for a long time. And for a while it was as though *that* part of Flo's life was done. The mothering part.

But. Sometimes Teddy calls. It's easier now that Flo at least lives in one place. She has a landline; Teddy can reach her, when she wants to reach her. And there are Teddy's letters. This card, for example.

I'm coming, it says in her peculiar slanted hand. It was like the handwriting of a child. Or a very old woman.

Take your pick.

63

Two winters passed, the second longer than the first, so that the snow around the river grew deeper than anyone could remember. The summers in between grew shorter and shorter, and sometimes Ksenia could hear the baying of the creature. The sound especially carried at night.

She was in the wilderness. This was her life now.

"The work is satisfying," Ksenia said as the second year drew to a close. ("Maybe she was building Hoover Dam," Teddy said once when Flo told her this story.)

"Go on," the witch always said next.

"It's good to work hard . . . ," Ksenia continued. Her voice trailed off; she wanted to see what the hag had to say.

The old witch cocked her head and regarded Ksenia. "You are like me," she finally said, gesturing to her face with its two eyes, her hands, her feet. "Not a beast. You are like me."

"I ***am*** *a beast," Ksenia thought. But she didn't say this out loud.*

64

Flo no longer thinks of her human self as being her best self. The things people were capable of! As far as Flo is concerned, being an animal might actually be something to aspire to, an improvement, though she understands she might be in the minority on this. She isn't daft.

In her mind, now, Flo runs through the ways in which animals are superior to humans. They:

- Provide unconditional love.
- Live in the moment.
- Never judge.

She does this to keep her mind off her ankle.

But some pain—physical, emotional—cannot be ignored. The pain in Flo's ankle can no longer be ignored.

Flo clambers out of the culvert. There is an Urgent Care, just there, in a strip mall that once held promise. The Urgent Care is sandwiched between a deli and a liquor store. Flo and Dog have passed it many times but until now Flo has not needed it.

A covered walkway fronts the strip mall, and there is one garbage can, overflowing with empty coffee cups and tiny green plastic bags—distended, knotted—filled with dog waste. When she limps inside, the Urgent Care is humble but sparkling clean. The rug is industrial, the chairs gray plastic. The air conditioning works, that's for sure.

"I hurt my ankle," Flo tells the young woman at the front desk. The woman has a nametag that says "Cal"; her hair is dyed pink. She is reading a book when Flo comes in, but she puts it down and smiles so genially that for a moment Flo feels great happiness. She imagines this Cal and her being friends in another life, the life beyond the blue door. Another opportunity, Flo thinks. She can picture telling Cal about SilverGirl, about Dog. Showing the young woman pictures, even.

It is good to have friends of all ages. Flo understands this suddenly: how it's good to have younger friends because people leave you. Whether they want to or not.

"You've come to the right place," Cal says, and she gives Flo a form to fill out. Her arm is tattooed with a dense sleeve of what look like mollusks and alligators. The tattoo is ugly but expert, and Flo admires the younger woman's confidence.

Flo props her branch against the wall and chooses a chair. She sits, she fills out the form. Someone has scratched the word *damned* into the gray plastic of the seat and Flo moves her leg over this. The Urgent Care is empty save for a stocky man with a port-wine stain on his face and his companion, a crying woman, hand wrapped in a bloody rag. The woman is making precise, repetitive gestures with her good hand and Flo tries not to stare. When a nurse calls them in, Flo waits to see what will happen. (Sunby might already know what will happen next, wherever he ended up. And SilverGirl surely does, she knows everything. Does Dog? Wait and see, Flo tells herself.)

Cal has gone back to reading her book, a romance novel. Flo doesn't know anything about romance novels and wishes she had something to say to this young woman, with her tattoos, her warmth. After a short period of time, during which Cal reads and Flo holds out her good foot, twisting it this way and that, the couple emerges. The woman is wiping her cheeks with a tissue, and the man has his arm around her. Her hand is neatly bandaged; no sign of blood anywhere.

Flo nods at them as they pass. "Blood freaks me out," the woman is saying to her companion. She doesn't notice Flo;

she's eating a cracker and drinking from a tiny wax cup of juice. She looks happier, she's not crying. Her hands, both of them calm, are as surprising as mittens in July.

Flo might like a cracker. She might like some juice. The couple walk out of the Urgent Care and Flo thinks, I will never see you again.

She takes Teddy's card out; she reads a few more lines. "I will see you soon," Teddy promises. Then the nurse calls Flo's name, looking neither kind nor unkind. She seems a little bored (though she *is* glamorous, her lipstick being an imperial shade of red). The doctor is more engaged. Flo gets an X-ray and then the doctor wraps Flo's ankle with a thick elastic bandage; she has a light touch. They are in a little cubicle with no windows and a curtain for a door.

"Did I go and break one of my pins?" Flo smirks. Her attitude, of course, is meant to hide her fear (*Don't ask the question you don't want the answer to*). But it's a sprain, thank gods, that's all. "Can I still walk?" she asks the doctor. "Today?"

"I'd take it easy," and the kind way the doctor says this, Flo has trouble swallowing. *Don't cry,* she tells herself sternly.

"I lost my dog," she finally manages. "I have to go find him."

"I see," the doctor says. Up close like this, her youth is apparent. She has acne. Her forehead is a little greasy.

Flo tells the doctor then about Dog: what he looks like, the orderly teeth and red fur. "He has a black tongue!" Flo says. Is this something she's imagined? No, she is pretty sure this is true.

"Good luck with that. But I'd advise you to take it slow."

"Can I have a cracker?" The doctor looks surprised, but nods. The crackers, individually wrapped in plastic, are kept in a cabinet along with bottles of hydrogen peroxide, and for a moment Flo is in her own fairy tale, receiving gifts the way the three daughters did. Flo puts the wrapped cracker into her skirt pocket along with Teddy's card. ("You have a dog now," Teddy wrote. "I always wanted a dog.")

Flo closes her eyes. She is actually having a hard time picturing the different parts of Dog, how they all fit together. She opens her eyes. Dog did not have fleas. He does not. Of this she is certain, and in this way she had (she has!) taken good care of him.

Flo slips off the examination table and stands before the doctor, arms folded because it is always so hard to know what to do with her hands. "You know, I'm afraid something bad may have happened," she says.

"Your ankle will be fine."

"To my—"

The doctor raises her hand. She reaches out and almost touches the scaly patch on Flo's neck. "What are you doing for this eczema?" she asks. "It looks inflamed."

"I'm keeping it at bay. I use a cream. Sometimes it works. Sometimes things work." Flo nods. "But I keep waiting to feel better, you know? I keep waiting for things to be all right?"

"It's pretty angry-looking," the doctor says. She looks at Flo, shrewdly. "Are you eating enough?"

"Oh, sure."

"Have you been depressed?"

"I'm fine!" Flo says. She had wanted to talk to the doctor, but not about this. She might have imagined a conversation like the ones she used to have with Sunby: What is a sprain, exactly? What is the difference between physical and emotional pain? What is *love*? But that would have been a conversation between friends.

The doctor nods. "If you need a different cream, come see me. Maybe I can help." She shrugs, still friendly enough.

"Can I have another cracker?" Flo asks. "I'm not usually like this," and the doctor pulls aside the curtain before wordlessly passing over a second cracker packet, and then another.

In the waiting room Flo's branch waits for her, a magic wand. It feels good in her hand again; she stops by Cal's desk.

"Thanks," she says. "I have to go find my dog now. He's missing." Flo gestures to her foot, the staff. "I didn't expect *this* to happen."

"You'll be okay," Cal says. She's put her book to one side; on the cover a man and woman embrace. There are boobs, there are abs. "I'm sure your dog will, too."

"Do you like that book?" Flo longs to cross the threshold of this (maybe) blue door. On impulse, she asks, genuinely curious, "Is it about love?"

Love being so resistant to definition.

Cal laughs. "Oh, not love! Not really. It's just . . . comfort food." Cal pauses. "But we get our comfort where we can, don't we? And love is a comfort, so, who knows, right?"

There must be something in Flo's face because the younger woman adds quickly, "He'll be okay. The dog. Don't forget, dog is god spelled backwards." Cal winks at her. "That can only be lucky, right?"

"Then it would be lucky for every dog," Flo says slowly. Reasonably. "Wouldn't it?" She touches the crackers in her pocket, thinking of juice. "Could I have something to drink? Like what that woman got?"

"Sure thing, hon." Cal gets up and disappears into the back. When she returns she holds a tiny cup of juice. It's red and sweet and Flo drinks it like you drink a shot. It's better than a shot.

"Here," Cal says. She presses a biscuit into Flo's hand. "We keep them for the service animals. Give it to your dog when you find him."

"I will." Maybe Flo really will see this Cal again. Maybe she will come back and tell Cal that she has found Dog, and that she has cats, too, and this: that she has a child. That she is trying to understand her child.

The door was still open, just a little.

But it's cold in the Urgent Care and, slipping the biscuit into her other pocket, Flo is happy enough to get back outside. The growing heat, in this moment, it feels good. She unwraps the crackers and nibbles at them so that they last. One and one and one. Salty flats, and she mashes them against the roof of her mouth.

Thank you, Flo says to the crackers. It is a conscious decision, allowing herself, as she does, to deserve the kindness of them. Perhaps they will fill her up after all.

She's tried her best. Flo has.

Sunby told her about transubstantiation once. Sunby! Flo says.

65

Ksenia remembered her mother's admonition, to be in the world and not of it, and she remembered her mother's counsel, to be patient, and she took comfort from the creatures of that forest, who came to her when she toiled alone and kept her company: gentle deer and keen foxes, red birds of the air and the grizzled squirrels. They loved her and she them. Ksenia used the remaining shells that she had gathered long ago, stringing them onto lengths of vine to make cunning bracelets and collars and even earrings. Shot through with a mineral blue, the shells were hard to describe. They were that beautiful. And if it was strange to see a deer with an earring looped over one delicate pinna, it was no stranger a sight than Ksenia herself, weighed down with her own garlands of shell. Her earrings.

She positively clinked when she moved. She was also a creature.

66

A DELIVERY VAN trundles by, and a truck coated in dirt almost to the windows so that it looks dipped. On the driver's door someone has written with a finger, in the dust: Dirty Dog. Flo's face and arms and calves are also gauzy with dust. With sweat. Once in a while there are voices—a lifting call, a childish voice answering. Flo stops and listens, head tilted. She imagines turning a knob, lowering the volume. She whistles for Dog.

One time she and Dog passed a red hawk, tearing at breakfast by the side of the road. That gleaming eye. Flo and Dog watched her eat and the hawk allowed it, though she would not be interrupted. Flo felt calm then. Teddy was the hawk, she thought. No: Teddy was the creature she was. She is. Flo told Sunby this the next time they talked on the phone.

"I have faith in Teddy," Sunby said.

"What if I stop loving her?" Flo asked.

"You won't," Sunby said tranquilly. "I have faith in you, also."

Flo does not return to the culvert. She is close enough to The Place now; she sticks to the sidewalk, passing a vacant lot that is gravel except for a pile of shattered glass that someone has thoughtfully swept together. She thinks about Sunby and is relieved she can still picture his face. She doesn't cry.

Instead, she focuses on the pain in her ankle, which might be the one true thing.

PART THREE

67

It was on the third day of the third winter when they heard the creature crying out, as was his custom. His voice was nearer now, and then he came into the clearing; Ksenia saw how the witch stiffened. The creature had changed—having grown to the height of three men—and he bade the witch to meet him at the river again.

"Ksenia has served her time," he said gravely. He laid out bread and cheese for sup; the witch ate quickly, growing to his height so that they were well matched. They left the clearing together, creature and witch, even as the creature caught Ksenia's eye and nodded. (Little Flo always loved this part. "What does the nod mean, Mama?" she would ask. And again: "What does it ***mean****?" Flo's mother always laughed and hugged her daughter close, saying, "His look told her, 'See, I have come. I always do.'")*

Ksenia hastened after them, in time to see the contest, with the witch straddling the river, holding her blackthorn aloft, and the creature standing tall. All the lightning from the heavens played around them both.

68

Back when Flo was employed at the community college in Ephrem, the ginger who worked Alumni Relations said that God only ever gave her what she could handle. Flo thought that was the stupidest thing she had ever heard. "Oh, just you wait," she'd said. "You can't even imagine."

This was shortly before Flo left that place. And she wasn't very nice when she said it. But she'd just about had it, hadn't she?

Flo is very close now.

She walks through an industrial park. All the buildings look more or less the same: flat, gray, laid out in tidy rows like Monopoly hotels. Sunby used to love Monopoly. Limping, she passes metal doors big enough for the semis to pass through, doors that shuffle open and closed. There are sidewalks for pedestrians. Which means only Flo.

The industrial park is arranged along a wide U-shaped street, which bows deep, the arms of the U swinging up into two entrances connected to the main road. At the bottom of the U a rutted clay track branches down from the street, cutting between a company called PowerHouse Steel Bearings and a shuttered dance studio. Flo leaves the order of the industrial park and follows the track, which passes a gravel pit, what Flo's mother used to call a borrow pit. "They use the gravel for construction," she would say. "They borrow the gravel so it can become something else."

Rain comes seldom here; the ruts of the track are baked into cement, cut deep in the clay. Flo follows these ruts carefully in her red shoes. The pain in her ankle is a bright star.

69

Beyond the gravel pit is a fence. Flo throws her staff over, then slips through a new gap in the chain-link, careful not to put another hole in her shirt. Now the fence is between her and the rest of the world. She holds her hands to her face; there is a metal smell on them.

The Place is bounded by the river on the other side; today the water is a flat silver band. There are no birds today, though in the past Flo has seen Cooper's hawks. Sometimes there is a wedge of egrets, spearing lizards for their dinner as is their nature. There are no benches to sit on. No winding path or playground equipment, no wet pour rubber protecting the ground. There is the fence to squeeze through or climb over, and scrub, which screens this stretch of the river from view. Sometimes trash collects against the outside of the fence. But there is rarely garbage on the inside here, near the river: when Flo thinks of it she brings a plastic garbage bag to pack any trash out, though she did not do so today.

She has never seen another person here. But today there was the new gap in the chain-link. Someone, something, has pushed its way through. Dog? She whistles for him. She imagines his loping run.

70

The hag howled.

The wind was roaring now, whipping up the water, and at one time it seemed as though the creature walked on the waves. Fish were leaping out of the way and thunder rolled, and the creature drew close enough to block the blackthorn's swing. The hag was strong, but the creature was stronger. When he threw the accursed blackthorn aside, he broke it, and Ksenia could hear the earth crack.

She put her hands to the sides of her head and the earrings she'd made were gone. Ksenia hardly registered their loss, although some time later, when she returned to this place, she would find them exactly where they had fallen. They would wait for her, and although most things—the forest, the world, Ksenia herself—would be different, the earrings would be the same. They would be a reminder of what had been, how far she had come.

71

Picking up her staff, Flo whistles again. "Dog!" she cries. When she finds him she will name him, she swears it.

The teacher's name was Jolene Benedict. Flo can't remember what the woman looked like, though the papers must have run a photo. It was only later she understood that, linked to Teddy and Jolene Benedict as she was, she, Flo, became part of a terrible happening in the town.

Honestly? She has never understood the events of that day.

- Teddy was so unhappy then.
- Her daughter's frontal lobe wasn't fully developed, was it?
- And hadn't the teacher said something unkind about her, Flo?

Nothing can explain what took place, of course. And it could have been all of these things, or none of them. Even Teddy doesn't seem to know, now, what she was thinking at that moment—or even during the whole of the year that preceded it. Just that she didn't mean to hurt anyone, least of all Mrs. Benedict, who in her awkward way had tried to take interest in a child she thought was broken.

Or neglected. There weren't many secrets in a town like Ephrem, and Flo had heard that the Benedict woman found Flo's smoking habit not only distasteful, but irresponsible. Flo's tendency to blow off parent/teacher conferences probably didn't help, or her offhand way of dressing. Flo heard from reliable sources that the Benedict woman found her peculiar. And it was true, Flo was markedly different from the mothers of Teddy's classmates, many of whom socialized, along with their respectable husbands, with the Benedicts outside of school.

At the time Flo took pride in her differences, even as she'd been offended by Mrs. Benedict's opinion of her. A few weeks before the incident, Flo might have even said something pointed to Teddy—"That woman looks down on us—can't you see that?"—and she can hardly think of that now, she doesn't want to look too closely at how jealous, how suspicious, she, Flo, had been when she said it. Jealous of the Benedict woman. Suspicious that maybe Teddy felt she needed another mother figure. That Flo wasn't enough. Of course after the incident Flo only felt horror, and her desire that Teddy and Mrs. Benedict had never met meant something different entirely.

Flo will never know what Mrs. Benedict said to Teddy that day. She will never know how the woman really saw Teddy, or if what Mrs. Benedict saw was even the truth.

What Flo does know is this: a week, or maybe it was a month before Teddy killed her teacher, impulsively swinging a length of fiber cement trim at the woman's head in Jolene Benedict's own backyard, Flo went walking in the woods. Her house had smelled stale. The politics at work were exhausting, and she was tired of the television. There were fields then, near the subdivision where she and Teddy lived. Perhaps those fields are there still. And beyond them, the woods.

The woods smelled juicy that day. It was the pines. Flo followed a path worn by countless local children, which led to a clearing, and in the clearing she saw her daughter. Teddy never knew her mother was there. She was in the clearing, walking on all fours. Her spine so cleanly straight. Like a fox, like a cat. ("I always wanted to *be* a dog," Teddy's card said.)

Proud and agile, Teddy moved around the open space with a look of concentration on her face. It was not unlike the time when, after a stayabed, Flo slipped into the living room and there Teddy was, she must have been seven. She'd lined up her stuffed animals—Cheetah and the teddy and a cat with fur grown mossy from wear—on the couch. They gazed back at her, light reflecting off their plastic eyes in crescents, in parabolas. Teddy bowed to them slowly, each in turn. Flo held her breath and backed out of the room, unwilling to break this moment.

It's hard to remember now, given what came after. But among those trees that passed for forest in Ephrem, white gloss of snow still on their branches, Flo felt bright strands of joy knit deep within her. You don't usually know, Flo understands later—years later, after Teddy had gone to Juvie and the shape of their lives had changed forever—the last time something happens. In its purest form.

72

Then the creature came to Ksenia, as in a dream. His brown eyes were clear, and the blue eye shone forth brighter than any sun. "Come with me," he said.

It took Ksenia a moment to understand: after all this time, the hag was dead.

Now the river was a dark rainbow, with a blaze of silver in its deepest crease. On the side where Ksenia stood with the creature, hand against his furred flank, the grasses were tall and green. The trees drooped with jeweled fruit and flowers big as platters, pink and red. On the far side the trees were stark, cutting their shapes against the sky like black lace, and leaves were on the ground, bronze and copper and gold. Ksenia understood that beyond the river was the land of the dead. She felt a heavy calm within herself, and she was not afraid.

"When do we cross it?" Ksenia asked.

The creature studied Ksenia with its great wise eye. "You are not Ksenia," he said. "You are Theodora." ("Did he call her Teddy for short?" little Flo used to ask. "Maybe," her mother said. And if Flo wished that Ksenia's real name was Flo she never said or let herself think it. She knew even then that sometimes the same thing can be called by many names.)

73

A MAN. From behind that hackberry there, he emerges, unsmiling.

There is something about him, but at first, Flo is just curious. Did he crawl under the fence? Is that dirt on his knees? Surely he's too old to be a threat, hat like a crushed cake, and where it's pushed back Flo can see the dimmest paste of hair over a lumpy red forehead. He wears a white suit, like a Southern gentleman, but it's yellow as teeth. His jacket has a raised moldy crescent on the breast pocket, too. And then, oh! Maybe it's grubby pajamas he has on.

I know you, Flo thinks.

"Hello," she says, and then she sees Dog. The man has him by the scruff, and there it is: she feels the first glitter of fear.

She is also off balance, as when you take a bite of something and you think it might be sweet. Butter, for instance, and the surprise when it's rancid, when you have to spit it out.

He's big. Bigger than she remembers, in front of his immaculate house with the porch and the cloud eye. The man here, at The Place, takes up a lot of room, heat seeming to rise off him in flat waves, and when she steps nearer he stares right through her. Dog is wriggling in his grip.

"Dog!" she cries. How glad she is to see him!

But the man's hand grips Dog's scruff, and when Flo gets closer she sees that the man's eyes are slitted at her, incurious. Dog's eyes, though: they are rolling, whites showing, and he twists in the man's grasp, those perfect teeth bared.

("It's time I met your dog," Teddy's card had said. "Don't you think?")

Flo stops, waiting, and when the man doesn't move she backs up a step. Be calm, she thinks. She passes the staff to her left (dominant) hand.

When the man smiles it's not a kind smile. His small eyes are like raisins in a bun, squeezed close together, and shiny. Then he is saying something—I told you to get rid of this thing—and his voice is genial; Dog's fur rises, a dorsal fin, all down his back. That's when Flo knows unequivocally to be afraid.

There had been a hurricane named after her. In 2018. That great bowl of wind and water, the destruction of it, bearing her name: gods the world was strange. Nature could be destructive, but it dispensed its luck, bad or good, dispassionately. Human beings though. The way they ended things. There was intention there, or there could be.

Flo is afraid of endings, she is! She and Sunby have talked about this and she wanted to tell Sunby now: about the hurricane, about the man.

Gods she misses him. She misses Teddy. Terribly. And in this moment, suddenly, she misses the person she used to be.

74

Satisfied with her name, her true name, Theodora returned the creature's gaze, and this time she was able to look into the blue eye, unafraid. He reared back then on his shaggy haunches. He stretched, and with his diamond hooves he removed his own head with its great hinged jaws. He did this as you might unscrew a jar, laughing and pulling. Then he shrugged from his hairy coat. Theodora blinked, and in that time the creature shrank down to the size of a man. He **was** *a man, though still with the third eye, which shone its hot, unflinching blue.*

"I am Death," he told her, "but we have time yet."

75

Flo has always thought she would die of cancer, tumors latching onto and in her, the sick cells spilling through first her stomach and then her liver, pushing and multiplying. So strange that this is how Sunby went.

But she still has time.

Before now, Flo never inspired fear the way Teddy did. Sometimes, maybe, she was not taken seriously.

When? She asks Dog this.

Now, Dog says.

She doesn't scream. Her fear seems to fill her with air; she feels that lightness back of her head, like falling, and the colors of The Place change rapidly. They were every shade of green and now Flo's Place is washed in amber, the river dazzled with an uproar of gold light. It is as if someone has poured paint into it. There is the Dog's yip—Stop hurting!—and the man's face so round and tight. Flo swings hard. Blood from his mouth, crimson threads flying out from where Flo catches him with the ring, the cut of the blue stone, and when she swings her staff, his head jolts to one side, he roars with pain. It is his song.

She wants to live. Even if Teddy never comes, even if it's only postcards from here on out. The sun lowers red and hard into the river and the trees near the river are black. Later, there's a spreading bruise black as the trees, black as ink on her buttock where the man kicked her. *He kicked her.*

"Blue!" Flo cries out without thinking.

He bit the man, then. Flo's skirt, swirling. Crepitating.

The man, running. And Flo and Dog: they got away, didn't they.

Flo believes that our animals are like us, that they grow with us, almost becoming us. Or we, them. But we never own another being.

76

(And here is the part Flo added, after The Place, after the man. It wasn't the end of the story, which she kept almost the same as her mother's telling. It was just before the end. It was her own.)

"You are endings, then." There was something in Theodora's voice, she couldn't keep it out.

"No. Don't be afraid. Think of me, if it helps—" and here the creature paused, his three eyes kind. Theodora knew herself to be understood. And she felt as if no harm could come to her, not now or ever.

"Think of me as change," the creature said.

Theodora did not completely understand him—she barely understood herself—but she loved him. And she knew she was loved in return. Together they retrieved her staff made of hazel, from where she had hidden it all those years before.

77

When Flo first visited Teddy in Juvie, there was a shyness to her, there was a shyness to them both. But she went. She did. All those years ago.

When Flo comes away with Dog there is a shyness to him. He doesn't run up right away when she calls to him—*Here boy!*—and she wonders fleetingly what might have happened to him in this short time. She brushes the thought away, not wanting to know. He bumps toward her, moving hard on his right front paw. He's been hurt, then, like her. They are alike. Here he is.

She runs to him and her ankle hurts in its wrap; the red shoes slip. She goes down hard, catching herself with her hands. When she puts her arms around Dog, her scraped palms streak his fur with clocks of blood. We're all right, she says.

Dog, he is so much sturdier than she remembered!

She pulls Cal's biscuit from her pocket and Dog eats it quickly and neatly. There is a merry sound to it, crunching.

Thank you, he says sincerely. I knew you would come. His tongue flickers pink.

What is your name? Flo wonders.

But it occurs to her, she always knew it.

One thing about Teddy: even in Florida, with those girls, she had kept her pride. She had her pride when she left Juvie, too. She had managed to outmaneuver these places and the people she found there.

She had the brass.

She was never broken. *Neither am I,* Flo thinks.

First there was the promise of the river. Then there was the river.

It was time to go home.

Flo touches the card in her pocket. Teddy's card. It's still there.

And Flo herself. Still there. Different, but also? The same.

Tumbleweeds of fur blow gently across the floor in the small breeze Flo makes, opening the door. The air smells like the incense she burns, and B. is home—Flo can hear her moving around. Now the cats crowd in, pushing around her legs, glad to see her and even the dog, Blue, who dips his head with his new mastery and reserve.

Blue had once lived a happy life, elsewhere. He wore a pink leather collar, he slept in a soft bed. Things changed. They changed again. But this life, in its way, is also good.

When Teddy was a very little girl, they adopted the cats Ender and Mars. Flo's mother was visiting them in Bakersfield; they went together to the animal shelter, a low tan building made of concrete blocks. The idea was that a cat would be a gift from Teddy's grandma. Well, they ended up getting two cats: the gregarious Mars and then there was Ender.

Ender was less than a year old but had already been adopted once; the woman at the shelter said that the family had gone on and gotten a dog, or had a baby, one or the other. The family brought Ender back, they didn't want him anymore. Flo thought that was shameful and she picked that cat up, boxy thing that he was. The cat nuzzled her and the shelter woman expressed amazement, because that wasn't, as she said, typical behavior for this cat. It was true: Ender was smart, and knew how to work his way in.

He wasn't a cuddly cat when they got him home. But they

loved him, and they were a family: Charlie and Flo and Teddy and both cats, with Flo's mom visiting the way she did. It was like a picture, almost. Anything seemed possible, and Flo thought, at that time, that it could always be that way. Or maybe it really *was* a picture, and Flo didn't remember the way it had been.

Of course Ender and Mars are probably long dead. They stayed with Charlie and now they are gone, as Charlie is gone. Flo's mother is dead, as is the world they inhabited together. And now Sunby. But Flo is alive. Teddy is. The man at the river, the man with the immaculate house: he is alive, too, but Flo never learned his name. She changes her phone number (*safe from the bastard*, she thinks); she will not pass his house again. There are other routes. She knows what happened with the man was true. She is not absolutely positive it was real. Perhaps this will make it easier for her to forget him.

His purpose having been served. It was not him, Flo understood, it was not the cloud eye, she needed to forgive.

The last sentence of Teddy's card is written in Derrykin. "Mother," Teddy writes. *Mother.* Then she says:

m&j% d%tstv* j% h&t&v%

Flo's Derrykin is rusty. At first she thinks Teddy is telling her:

My childhood was shit.

But maybe what she really meant was:

My childhood is done.

Flo puts a hand against the wall for balance as the animals move around her. They adore her, she understands suddenly, and she adores them in turn. Flo rubs her ankle in its wrap.

And here is the magazine she was reading, left open on the couch. Somewhere water is running, yipping as it does, and Flo looks at Blue conspiratorially. He doesn't yip. He never did.

Here she is.

Flo takes the room in, greedily. This morning she'd pulled the blinds down against the promise of day's roaring light. She opens them now. Soon this day will end. Flo will make the tea she likes, lumpy with old powdered cream. Perhaps she will take the secret passage to visit B., and she will shout out, and together they will look out at the moon, the way it sips the sky. Its silver light.

Teddy's hair was the white of the moon. She will arrive in a week, a month. She will bring her own strange story. She might be bitter. But perhaps she will be happy. Perhaps she will smile her provisional smile, bringing out the shell earrings that Flo thought she'd lost. Maybe Teddy has been holding on to them all this time; Flo imagines the sheen of those earrings. The reassuring weight of them.

But she cannot figure what *will* in fact happen, which is this: when Teddy arrives she will give her mother a gift. She will tell Flo the key to Derrykin.

It's Czech, Teddy will say, Derrykin is. Czech-*ish*. Because Teddy had been so little when she made this language. "I tried to start from scratch," she will say. "But it was all gibberish. It was too hard for me." And so Teddy, small as she was, pored over the Czech/English dictionary gathering dust on her mother's shelf of books. It was a place to start and she was clever, she replaced the vowels. With symbols! "I disguised it, I wanted it to be our own," Teddy will say, and Flo will assure her, "It was, it *is*."

"It was meant just for you." Because here is the thing: Teddy thought it might be nice—for both of them—to speak something like Flo's grandfather's tongue.

And Flo's heart? That day, there will be no name for what she feels.

"I should have told you sooner. About Derrykin. If you know where something comes from, it's easier to understand." They will be eating cupcakes together, sparkly ones, with pink frosting, and also pale blue. What a relief, to be eating together. "Sometimes, at least," Teddy will add.

This is what will happen. But Flo can't know that, not yet, that story is still waiting to be told.

Scritch scritch. Flo reaches down to scratch Blue's neck. She scratches at her own. She wonders if she will ever outgrow this eczema. We are always changing, the doctor said.

But there is the real question. Why don't I just give her up? Flo wants to know.

You won't, Blue says.

Why can't I let her leave me?

The animals chorus: mothers and children, they burn in each other.

N#k&n%c js%m t% n%ztr#t*l

(I didn't lose you after all.)

78

Theodora and Death returned to the red mountain so that they might marry. Theodora's mother was at the wedding, of course, joyful and relieved because we never know, do we, if what we give has been enough. And if she wondered about her daughter's unusual connection with Death, she also understood that Theodora was creating her own path, informed in ways both beautiful and painful by the life she had lived so far.

Maybe Theodora's mother had a clearer sense of what it meant to be her daughter. Maybe she had a clearer sense of what it meant to be herself. In any case, here they both were. Both of them different than they had been, but also the same. Connected.

And Theodora's sisters came with their husbands and their children. The wizard was also there; if he was not handsome, he was still a beautiful sight to Theodora, who had come so far. She had thought she might never see him again. (The day after The Place, after the man, Flo will finish her story for B. Listen! she will say. There the wizard was. Someday Theodora would have to learn how to carry him in her mind's eye, fire in a horn. But that was another day, not yet come. They weren't there yet.)

And the rest of the story was always the same, wasn't it? There was a great wedding feast on the mountain, with platters of food from the ground and the air and the sea and the fire. No one had ever seen the like.

There was joy.

79

AND JUST AS little Flo had done, B. will cry: "Tell me the joys!"

Some things cannot be listed, Flo's mother used to say. Some things cannot be named. We try to impose order, but—and here Flo's mother would laugh. You'll see. You'll see in time.

Flo's mother would kiss her daughter then.

Some things can only be accepted, she would say.

Flo, in her living room, with her animals. She rises and goes with Blue to the closet. She opens the laundry bag and there are Teddy's photos.

Let things be what they are, her mother said. Okay, let things be what they are, B. will concede.

You aren't alone in it, Blue adds.

80

And everyone (except the hag, wherever she had gone) was happy. Glasses were raised, again and again. The feast, with all its food and its merriment, its music and joy, didn't end after an hour or even a day. It didn't end after a year.

Truth be told, it may be going on still.

Is it still going on? Flo asks Blue, and SilverGirl. She asks the clowder of cats. Who knows? they reply. We hope so.

81

WHEN TEDDY LEFT Lead Grove, she'd called Flo on the phone. This was when she'd said corn packing wasn't for her. They had talked about Hoover Dam.

"I love you," Flo told Teddy, at the very end of that conversation. How had Flo forgotten this? In spite of everything, it was true then. It was true, still. Sunby had been right all along.

"I love you," Flo had said, and they were both quiet. This was not uncomfortable. It wasn't sad, either. "I don't know when you and I will see each other next." Flo's life is unlike anything she has planned for. Teddy's life is unlike the lives of anyone she knows. "I will miss you always," Flo said, and this was true also.

We'll see, Flo tells the animals now. She is very still. It is as though her whole life passes through her. Joy pinwheels in her breast, a Catherine wheel. She's made fresh starts before.

The blue door, there it is.

D&K&NČ*T

SHE WONDERS if she will ever return to the river; sometimes she asks Blue this. She says she thinks she might choke the river with stones, set the surrounding scrub alight. But she might also sit on its edge, finally set her feet in the water, coolness against an ankle that will always retain a phantom ache.

She might bring crackers to eat. She might bring some juice, or even wine. The light would come—flakes of silver, or gold, on the surface of the water. Light! The promise of that, of limitless ease. Some day. Another miracle. Everyone whole.

A time to rest? A time to rest, though it is only morning.

Who knows?

Teddy's Letter

Flo,

I'm coming to visit. You. Soon.

I could use some time with you, Flo. It's been a while since we've done anything together.

You should know. You should know that I have been on a journey. I've been lonely. I wish I had a blue door. I don't. Of course. But I've been north. I've been west. It's time for me to go deeper. I might be south soon enough, by ____, I reckon. I'm coming.

I've been thinking a lot about my childhood. You used to make me go shopping. What was that all about? I expected more from you. But that was me, at 14. When I was growing up, I didn't always like you. I guess you knew that. I guess in some ways Sunby was our go-between for a while. I miss him. I haven't heard from him lately. I know I'm hard to reach. I keep on moving. But when I get to the next place, I'm still the same.

You are settled, though. I will see you soon. You have a dog now. I always wanted a dog. I always wanted to *be* a dog.

It's time I met your dog. Don't you think?

I will see you soon. Mother. My childhood is done. [This last sentence is in Derrykin.]

~ Teddy

The Rules of Derrykin

The language is Czech, but with no vowels. Instead, make these substitutions:

- a = #
- e = %
- i = *
- o = &
- u = !

ACKNOWLEDGMENTS

In 2019, my friend Mary Jo Kanady suggested we attend an Off Campus Writers' Workshop (OCWW) class, about interwoven narratives, together. I thought it would be a fun evening—dinner with my good friend, then class—and it was. But when I signed up, I had no idea how inspiring the night would turn out to be. Memoirist/novelist Zoe Zolbrod taught the class, which focused on how multiple storylines can inform and deepen a narrative. I came away charged with the energy of this idea, and it percolated in my brain for two years before I found myself wanting to return to characters who'd appeared in my *Strange Attractors* collection. Flo in particular still had something to say, and it became increasingly clear that a braided storyline was a format that might play to her strengths. Thank you to Mary Jo and Zoe for helping Flo find her voice in this way.

The idea of dual storylines felt ambitious, and at times perplexing: it took me multiple stabs to refine a narrative that picked up Flo's story and incorporated a fairy tale her mother had told her as a girl. Ellen Akins, thank you for seeing the promise in those early pages, and for helping me realize what Flo's story could be. Katherine Shonk and Diane Kastiel: you likewise read an early draft of this book with generous spirits, insight, and attention; thank you for your encouragement and for feedback that elevated *The Blue Door* and helped me make discoveries about Flo in the drafts to come.

To John Hensler, Miriam Seidel, and Douglas Gordon: our brainstorming sessions as we imagined a cover that might do Flo and her storytelling justice were fun and inspiring. And huge thanks to all the folks at New Door Books: Doug, you believed in *The Blue Door* from the get-go, and your thoughtful feedback pushed me to further and better imagining; Nathaniel Popkin, my editor at New Door, you approached Flo's story with sensitivity, wisdom, and insight. Thanks to New Door Books and Sheryl Johnston, my intrepid publicist, Flo is making her way into the world again. I love working with you all.

This book was written at home, and at Spring Bird Cottage in West Dundee, Illinois, and the Write On residency program in Door County, Wisconsin. Thank you to Anna Lentz and Jerod Santek for creating such inspiring places for artists to imagine, create, and vibe with the local deer. My writing getaways with Sandra Jones and Katherine Shonk, in different Midwestern locales, also contributed significantly to the completion of this book, as did my coffeehouse writing dates with Kathy Bergen. Thank you, friends.

The following individuals have all inspired or advised as this book evolved, and I thank you with love: Conversations with Fran Dvorak, who observes life with candor and insight, have informed my idea of Flo and her friend B., both of them storytellers. Fran, the lens through which you view the world inspires my art, and my life. Conversations with loved ones over the years informed *The Blue Door* in sometimes unexpected ways: Annie Lepkowski, your gifts as a social worker, and our cherished weekly phone calls, energized me as I worked to better understand Flo's chosen profession of social work. Mary Sustar, our long walks and wide-ranging conversations about emotional logic—and life!—have informed these pages and uplifted my spirit. Special thanks, too, to

Jane Ervin, Christina Hoffmann, Anna Jóelsdóttir, Mary Kenney, Norman P. Kenney, and Kevin McCoy for your support during this book's evolution. You are all incredibly dear to me.

Finally, loving thanks to Fred Shafer, my writing mentor and friend, and to my extended family, for your support and belief in my work.

Marion, I love you. David, you are my touchstone and my rock; you have my love, always, and thanks for your belief in me as a human, and your celebration of the stories I tell.

WalkAbout

The **WalkAbout** series from New Door Books honors every kind of journey on foot, the epic and the everyday, the flight and the return, the perilous and the steady, as paths to encounters, discovery, and surprise. **WalkAbout** champions literature, both fiction and nonfiction, where moving at a human pace fosters close witness and heightened attention to the environment, the people around us, and the urgencies of our time.

Ways of Walking: Essays
edited by Ann de Forest

The Blue Door: A Novel
by Janice Deal